A Beautiful Idea

By: Emily McKee

D1707614

A Beautiful Idea

Copyright © 2013 by Emily McKee. All rights reserved.
First Print Edition: January 2014

Limitless Publishing, LLC
Kailua, HI 96734
www.limitlesspublishing.com

Formatting: Limitless Publishing

ISBN-13: 978-1494755782
ISBN-10: 1494755785

Dedication

For Matt:

Another star twinkling in the night sky. Another wisp of the wind along my face. Another wave crashing in the ocean. Another ray of light beaming down from the sun. Another drop of rain that falls from the sky. Another beautiful, ornate snowflake. Now, for the rest of my life whenever I see or feel one of these I will think of you.

"Everything begins with an idea."
-Earl Nightingale

Chapter 1

"You'll never amount to anything, you little bitch, so what's the point?" Cynthia said, holding the front door open for me. "You never have and never will amount to anything! All you've ever had are ideas. Look at where you are. Nowhere! Who are you? Nothing!" The second I stepped out onto the front porch the door was slammed shut behind me.

Cynthia is my mom. She sounded harsh, but it didn't really matter what she said. She could never make me feel half as bad as I already felt. She's been putting me down for as long as I can remember. At first, it was just little things here or there, but as I got older the words got worse.

It's not like she hit me or anything.

It was much worse.

She ignored me.

In a weird way, when she did talk to me, I was grateful, because half the time I felt like I was invisible.

I took a few seconds to catch my breath, grabbed my bags, and packed up my car. By packing up my car I mean putting a bunch of garbage bags filled with my prized and worldly possessions in the back of my shit automobile. After squeezing everything in there it took five minutes to slam the door shut. Sometimes the door on the back of the car got stuck.

Just my luck.

I was determined to start my new life, a junior at the University of Maryland. My motto with my mom was *outta state, outta mind* which is exactly why I decided to leave good ole New Jersey and make my way to Maryland.

Plus, I would finally see the beach! It wasn't like I had a huge fascination with the beach. I just wanted to see what all the fuss was about. I'd always read about how good the sand feels between your toes and the calming sounds of the waves rocking back and forth. But if you ask me, the beach sounded awful. Sand between your toes sounded annoying as well as gross.

After graduating high school, I took general classes at the local community college and worked at a grocery store to save up money so I could move out. Some girls smacked their gum and lost brain cells; I passed the boring time with my head in a good book.

I wasn't dealt the best hand in life. My mom was a junkie and my dad bailed when he found out she was pregnant with me. I liked to refer to him as "the sperm donor," and ever since then Cynthia has loathed me. Children's Services stepped in a couple of times and every time I was placed back into the "stable environment" of a crackhead alcoholic.

Huh, some legal system we have.

There were days and sometimes weeks when we didn't have electricity or sewer and I have been on food stamps for as long as I can remember. Let me just say that whoever invented powdered milk is a complete and total basket-case!

Anyway, Cynthia decided I was going to be her only mistake. So while there are families out there with numerous kids, I was all by myself. We were dirt poor, so I couldn't really do much, and in high school I kind of kept to myself. Sure, I had a few friends here or there, but nothing lasted. They never interested in sticking around. Plus, while kids were ditching class and getting drunk on the weekends, I was more interested in my books and steering clear of Cynthia's wrath.

So while most teenagers were sucking face, I had my head in the clouds or in a book. I'm an avid reader and when I read, I escape. The point to reading and watching movies are to escape your shitty, fucked up life for just a few hours. That was why, on the rare occasions when I did get to see a movie and it sucked big time, I made a point to complain until I got a refund. I didn't care that the girls were from my school and would make fun of me the following Monday morning. But anyway, back to why I read. I liked to think I was the leading lady getting the *Happily Ever After*.

My head was always filled with ideas and possibilities, but that's all they ever were. I decided a change was in order and I was going to make my dreams a reality. If you haven't figured it out yet, then you're a complete bonehead. I, Isabelle Katherine Clark, Iz for short, want to be an author.

I wanted to write about everyday people who live extraordinary lives. No, not like meeting a billionaire, but meeting a regular guy and falling in love, having the white picket fence, and 2.5 kids. I might throw in a serial killer to spice it up a bit, but you catch my drift.

We needed to get back to the times of Elizabeth Bennett and Mr. Darcy or Tristan and Isolde. Where you felt that life-altering, ground-breaking, universe-shifting true love. The simplicity of it that made me wonder if that could happen in real life. The events of my life up to that point had given me the answer. No, it couldn't.

Unfortunately, our stories and the paths we choose aren't written by authors who sit behind a computer desk and have all the time in the world to calculate the perfect words for answering a question or how we're going to throw ourselves at who we think is the love of our life. Nope.

We get one chance and that one chance can make or break us. Turn our event into enchantment or tragedy. Either tears are shed or the sounds of laughter fill a room.

We aren't able to click *backspace* or *delete.* That's the beauty of real life; good or bad we live in the moment.

After finally managing to slam my car door shut, I drove toward my new life. Driving through my hometown, I saw couples holding hands and children playing on the playground. Little did those people know that today my life became significant and I was no longer a wallflower. I was no longer nothing. I was going to be someone and do something with my life.

I drove the six hours to school with a huge ass smile on my face. I wasn't smiling because I was on my way to school to write papers, take tests, and do midnight cram sessions to study for finals. *Because what moron would be excited about that?*

No, I was excited to have a fresh start. Nobody knew me where I was going, so I could be anyone. Do anything. For all these people knew, I was a princess who'd decided she wanted a normal life and was done having the responsibilities of taking care of a country. Or better yet, I was a movie star. *Huh, yeah, I told you I had dreams and ideas.*

Of course I had to make a pit stop on the way to get a ginormous Dr. Pepper and my kryptonite, Swedish Fish. But finally, I arrived at the start of a new life. My new life.

Since I was a transfer student I got shitty housing and had to live with all of the freshmen because I didn't know anyone. I didn't complain though because anything was better than living with Cynthia, so I thank you, financial aid!

After pulling into a parking spot and turning off my car I sat and stared at all of the people around me.

It was kind of pathetic, really. Out of all the kids moving into their dorms, only I was all by myself. Lonesome. A loser. But then I saw a guy whose mom was choking the living shit out of him and getting mascara goop all over his shirt. Did I mention that some hot chicks walked by and giggled? What a poor bastard.

My situation wasn't that bad.

After finally quitting the people watching and moving in all my junk, I decided to walk around campus. After all of five minutes, I was completely bored out of my mind and headed back to my room. You know what I saw on that walk around campus? Buildings, buildings, more buildings, trees, grass, and did I mention buildings? I contemplated putting everything away but I was a procrastinator so I decided to wait until very late that night or the next day or never to organize my room.

The only good thing about my *adventure* was stopping at the cafeteria to pick up something to eat. I grabbed a sandwich because everything else scared the living shit out of me. *Who the hell eats raw fish? And what the hell is a wrap?* I figured a turkey sandwich on rye with pickles and a bag of chips was the safe choice.

After eating, I decided to sit on my bed and think about my life.

How it was.

How it would be.

While Cynthia and I only shared the common bond of hating one another, I still wanted to thank her. Without her being who she was I would have never decided to get the hell outta Dodge.

I hadn't put any of my stuff away and it was close to midnight. The only thing I did was make my bed and read a book. As soon as I got ready for bed, music blasted and the screaming and cheers began. *Ugh, just kill me now!*

Oh well, so much for my beauty rest.

***

Beep! Beep!

"Ugh!" Slamming my alarm clock, I grabbed my shower supplies and dragged my lazy ass to the bathrooms. Since I was lucky enough to schedule my classes later in the day, all of the hot water was gone thanks to the obnoxious early risers.

Back in my room, I looked around at four bare walls, an uncomfortable bed, and a big ugly brown desk with a chair to match.

"Well, Iz, so far nothing is different. The food sucks. The water is cold. It's loud as hell at night. If there isn't a difference within the next twenty-four hours, I'm going to be sooo pissed."

Then I thought of Cynthia and I realized I could never go back. It's not like she would miss me, but I couldn't take anymore of her comments. So while my life was similar in most aspects, I'd take it if it got me away from Cynthia.

After getting ready, I decided to check my emails. I skipped through all the nauseating greetings from professors and the resident advisor … My heart stopped on the email entitled *Student Financial Aid*. Taking a few deep calming breaths I clicked on the email.

Miss Clark,

I regret to inform you that there are a few errors with your financial aid. I need to clear a few things up, so when you have a chance today or tomorrow I would like you to come down to the Financial Aid Office.

Sincerely,
Patricia A. Alexander
Financial Aid Office
University of Maryland

"What the hell? All before a cup of coffee is in my hands! Wow, these people play dirty!"

I quickly checked my clock and saw that I had an hour until my first class, so I grabbed my bag and keys and made my way to the dining hall. If I was going to deal with people holding my future in their hands, I was going to need to have some coffee so I didn't freak out too much.

Well, just another thing to add to the shit list. Really, people? This is college! Was it a little too much to ask for some decent coffee?

After traveling across campus I finally made it to the Financial Aid Office and walked in.

"Hi, how can we help you?" the receptionist asked.

"Uh, I'm here to see Patricia Alexander."

"Okay, I'll inform her you're here. Please have a seat."

I sat down on the comfy couch and waited. I sat across from this guy who wasn't all that bad to look at and it dawned on me it was the same guy whose mom was choking him yesterday. Before I could hold it in any longer I started to laugh. He was looking down at his paper and then looked up at me. After taking a few calming breaths I got my bearings and decided to check out my schedule and the map I'd picked up on the way into the office.

I felt like the biggest dork, because you know exactly who the new kids are when they're too busy to make friends because they have their schedule and a freaking map in front of them.

A few minutes later an older lady came up to me. She looked nice enough. She was a few inches taller than me and about fifty pounds heavier. She had shoulder-length, salt and pepper hair and was wearing a purple sweater and grey dress pants. "Hi, you must be Isabelle Clark. Nice to meet you," she said, shaking my hand.

"Nice to meet you too, Miss Alexander."

I could feel my voice shaking and I probably should have wiped my hands on my jeans before shaking her hand, but no turning back now.

"Oh honey, call me Patty. Please follow me."

Wow, maybe this wasn't a problem at all. I could definitely weasel my way out of this one if they had a lady like Patty in charge.

I followed her into her office and looked at the pictures on her desk as she sat down and started up her computer. All were of her and her smiling family, which in turn made me smile. All the pictures were from different times in their lives. Ballet recitals and lacrosse games. Graduations from high school and college. First child.

I couldn't help but think her kids were real lucky to have parents who loved them that much.

I've never had anybody who has cared about me, much less loved me. My dad bailed, which in turn made Cynthia blame me and hate me. I never met any of my grandparents and, as far as I'm aware, Cynthia is an only child.

Breaking me from my thoughts, Patty said, "Please have a seat, Isabelle."

I took the chair closest to her desk and sat down. I put my bag on my lap and took a few much needed breaths.

"All right, Isabelle, it looks like there's a problem with your financial aid. It doesn't cover all of your room and board."

My heart stopped and my eyes bulged out of my head.

"What does that mean?"

"It means that you owe $5,000 by the end of this week or else you'll have to find a new place to live off campus. I'm sure it will be fine, Isabelle. Your parents can probably help you out and you can get a job on campus. Don't worry, it will all work out," she said with a genuine smile.

"Um, that's not possible."

"Oh honey, don't worry; there are a bunch of different job openings on campus. I can give you a list of places to visit today."

"No, I mean my parents helping out."

She stopped working on her computer and looked at me. I could see the sadness, but she quickly turned it into a bright over-achieving smile. "Well, let's just get the extension into action and I'll print you out those job openings. Now be aware that the extension will run out at the end of September."

I smiled and nodded.

I contemplated getting in my car and driving over to the gas station to pick up a lottery ticket.

Maybe for once the universe would be on my side but then I realized: oh you need money in order to buy a lottery ticket. Dammit!

No wonder they'd put a lady like Patty in charge of Financial Aid. She seemed like such a sweet lady and had the cutest voice ever. How could be anybody be rude to her?

After getting the list of job openings and thanking Patty, I left the office. There was still a half hour to kill so I decided to sit on a bench outside the café and look at the list of job openings.

1)   Spanish Tutor. *No, thanks.*
2)   French Tutor. *Maybe?*
3)   Athletic Department. *Hell to the No!*
4)   Librarian Assistant. *yes! Yes! YES!*

Well, that's a positive. At least I can actually get paid to read. How cool is that?

I thought about going to the library to put in an application, but decided that getting another cup of that *delicious* coffee was in order. Before I got up, I looked around to see if there was a quicker way to get to the cafeteria. That's when I noticed people were giving me weird stares.

I decided to just get up and get a move on. Plus, my butt was getting numb from the uncomfortable bench, another thing to bitch about.

After standing up and stretching, I prepared to make my way to the cafeteria. As I put the job listings in my bag, I felt somebody run into me.

Chapter 2

"Oh man, I'm sorry," he said while helping me up. I was about to bitch slap the asshole when I looked into his eyes. HOT DAMN! He had dark brown eyes and was drop dead gorgeous. He had sleeves of tattoos, piercings in his ears, and he was huge.

He was a lot taller than my 5'3" frame. At least 6'4". *Great, now I can't get the idea of how huge he is out of my head!*

Not to mention his body should be illegal. I didn't know half those muscles existed and I felt them up against me. He said something, but I, of course, had turned into an idiot.

Come on, Iz, think of something clever to say. Anything?

"Huh?"

Really, that's all you can say? You could at least say something with two syllables. After all, you want to be a writer.

"I asked you if you were all right, sweetheart," he said while chuckling at me and then he smiled. *And holy shitballs, motherfucker, he had dimples. Ugh. Yup, I was a goner! Long gone, sayonara sucker! Wait just a hot second. Did he just call me sweetheart? That's it. Sweetheart was going to kick his sweet little ass!*

"My name is Isabelle, but most people call me Iz, and I ain't your sweetheart, munchkin."

As I sidestepped him, he grabbed my arm and swung me around. I thought he was going to yell at me but I saw the biggest smile on his face. He said, "I'm Ryder Mitchell, or munchkin to you, and I think I just found my new best friend."

"Ryder?" I questioned. "What kind of name is that?" I blurted. *Oh my God, did I just say that out loud?*

Hearing a deep groan coming from the gorgeous guy, my eyes locked with his. Smirking down at me, he leaned in and said, "It's Ryder. Think of it as 'I'll ride her all night long,'" as he placed his hand out to shake mine.

My mouth dropped open and started to water. Butterflies soared in my stomach and I could feel my face becoming red.

As he stood there with his hand out, I could see people out of the corner of my eye stopping in their tracks and staring.

Did I have something on my face? Oh no, did I split my pants?

After my little internal freak out I looked up into Ryder's eyes. He stared right back at me and the look in his eyes made me feel safe. *Oh, what the hell.* I decided to just go for it.

I took his hand in mine and instantly felt shocks and jolts. I took a few seconds to breathe in and out because it felt like I was being brought back to life. After shaking the feelings off, I said, "Hi, Ryder. I'm Isabelle Clark, or sweetheart to you."

As I looked up into his dark brown twinkling eyes, I said a prayer.

Dear God, Buddha, Allah, (basically all gods out there in the universe),
I believe this Gorgeous Greek God will be the death of me!
Amen
P.S. Thank you!

"So, Isabelle, where are you headed?" he asked, still holding my hand. I smiled at the way my name sounded rolling off his tongue. Then I wondered what else his tongue was good at.

I just met the guy and I have never felt like this before, not even with the guys I 'dated' during high school. If you want to call going to the movies and being bored out of my mind 'dated.' I think paper-cutting myself to death or gouging out my eyes with a rusty fork would be better entertainment.

"Well, I was going to go to get another cup of this horrendous coffee and head to class, but I'm not sure I'll be able to do that with you still holding my hand," I said with a wink. At that exact moment he let go of my hand and I swear it felt like all the air left my lungs.

My mouth instantly turned down and I looked down at my hand. Even though he stood right in front of me, it felt like he was fifty feet away. I wanted him to touch me again, but I would take just hearing his voice talking to me.

For now.

Trying to clear my head, I looked back up at him through my eyelashes and I swear I saw him blush slightly.

"Well, I have an idea. I'll go with you and then walk you to class," he said. We walked to the café and he held the door open for me. *Huh, such a gentleman.* I swear as soon as we walked into the café the noise volume went down significantly and people were staring at us.

Seriously, was there something on my face?

After we got our coffees and left the café, the whispers turned up significantly and I swear all of the voices were saying something like Ryder this and Ryder that. *Seriously, who in the hell is this Ryder Mitchell?* I took a sip of my coffee and contemplated that as we began walking to my class.

The coffee wasn't that horrendous after all, at least not when Ryder paid for it. *I would gladly slurp that shit up all day, every day if he bought it for me.*

For a while the walk to class was silent but then Ryder started to talk. "So sweetheart, what class do you have right now?"

I shrugged my shoulders and pulled out my embarrassing paper with my schedule printed on it. I handed Ryder my cup of coffee. "Here, hold this."

I heard Ryder laughing. "I like a girl who's bossy." I shook my head and attempted to keep in the laughter that was building up. I needed to stay calm in front of this guy. I was already thinking about how huge he was and his tongue for Christsakes.

I scanned my schedule and told him that I had Creative Writing. After putting the paper back in my bag, I turned to get my cup of coffee and saw Ryder had a big smile on his face.

I took a sip of my coffee and then asked him what he was smiling about. He just shook his head and said, "Nothing."

Um, okay. Can you say awkward?

"So, Ryder, what class do you have?"

"Oh, I have a writing class in the same building."

The rest of the walk to our classes was silent. It wasn't one of those awkward silent walks, it was comfortable. I wanted him to say something more, but he never did. I was way too nervous to come up with anything. I just tried to calm the butterflies going crazy in my stomach. I had finally managed to get up the courage to start a conversation with him when we stopped at my Creative Writing class.

"Well, this is me. Nice to meet you again, Ryder, and thanks," I said with a smile.

He held the door open for me and I was half tempted to turn around just to see his fine tight ass shake down the hall as he walked away but I stayed as calm as I could. I chose a seat in the back because I absolutely loathed sitting in the front. Plus the only people who sit in the front are the obnoxious assholes who answer every damn question like they're on *Jeopardy!*. I slid into my seat and pulled a notebook and pen out of my bag. After straightening up, I saw that Ryder was sitting in front of me. He'd turned around to stare at me.

"Ryder, what are you doing here? You have to go to class."

He shrugged and had a sly grin on his face. "Well, the thing is, I'm kind of in this class, too. Surprise."

I thought I had finally managed to calm down all the butterflies, but with that grin and those damn dimples of his, they went wild and free.

When class was over we walked out together but a whole group of people came up to him and I was pushed into the background. Guys were high fiving him and girls were practically drooling and hanging on every word coming out of his mouth. I'd thought maybe he was different. He sure did make my body do crazy things on the inside but I looked at all the girls surrounding him and I was way, way out of my league. These girls were dressed in barely there skirts and tank tops that didn't cover up much of anything.

I just shrugged my shoulders. Oh well, back to my reality. At that exact moment my stomach started to grumble. Before settling this whole financial aid fiasco I decided to walk to the café and get something to eat.

As I was grabbing my sandwich a girl nudged me and said, "Ryder Mitchell hasn't taken his eyes off you since he walked in here." I turned to look at her. She had long, blonde hair and was a lot taller than me. She reminded me of a human Barbie doll and I swear she could be in a hair product commercial. Her hair was so shiny and looked like silk compared to my wavy brown mess of a rat's nest.

"Oh, Ryder is just a friend, we're in class together."

"Huh. Ryder isn't friends with girls. Especially girls like you," she said.

I couldn't believe this girl. "What exactly does that mean, Barbie?" I said with a bit of attitude.

She must have gotten my hint because she said, "Oh no, I think you got the wrong idea. What I mean to say is that you're gorgeous and you are so his and every other guy's type at this school. Hell, you're my type and I'm straight. I think we got off on the wrong foot. Hi, I'm Sarah Thompson."

I started to laugh and introduced myself. "I'm Isabelle Clark, but everyone calls me Iz or Izzy. Nice to meet you, Sarah."

After I paid for my sandwich and Sarah paid for her sushi I was ready to leave but Sarah grabbed me by the arm. "Oh no, you don't. Come on and sit with us." We walked to the back of the dining hall arm in arm, which kind of annoyed me. I wasn't used to that kind of thing. I was the last person to have girlfriends or any type of friend, really. Sarah stopped at the end of a long lunch table and started the introductions.

"Okay, guys, this here is Isabelle Clark. She's Ryder's new girl. Isabelle, this is everybody. The hottest twins known to mankind, Jason and Jade Williams; the naughty librarian, Ashlynn Miller;

and my sexy ass beast of a boyfriend, Gabe Prescott."

After all the introductions I sat at the end of the table next to Jade, who was really pretty. She reminded me of a Grecian goddess with her long brown hair with blonde highlights and darker complexion. Ashlynn Miller reminded me of the girl next door with her looks. She looked like one of those girls who don't even have to try. She could wear no makeup at all and still look really pretty. Jason looked like a freaking model with his looks. Hell, he was like 6'3" and had dirty blonde hair with a bit of scruff on his face that looked downright sexy as hell. It actually made my toes start to curl and the butterflies instantly swarmed around in my belly. Gabe had his head shaved and some tattoos up and down his arms. He looked like a badass, but the second he opened his mouth he reminded me of a giant teddy bear. Gabe was sweet and I understood why he and Sarah were together. He actually reminded me of another certain someone who had tattoos and piercings and I started to smile.

Everyone seemed pretty nice and they asked me all sorts of questions. After answering the basic questions …

Where are you from?

What's your major?

Why'd you choose University of Maryland?

… Everyone seemed to go back to normal. I couldn't help but notice how dreamy Jason was and I couldn't take my eyes off him. He was sitting right across from me and I noticed how his gaze flickered between Ryder and myself, but I didn't really think anything of it.

Seriously, people, can someone please, for the love of God, tell me if I have something on my face? Oh no. Do I have something in my teeth?

"So, Sarah, who exactly is this celebrity Ryder Mitchell that I keep hearing everybody talk about? Why were you so surprised that we were just friends?"

Sarah and Gabe were in their own little world whispering to one another. "Sweetie, Iz just asked you a question."

"Oh, Iz, I'm sorry. What'd you say?"

"No, it's okay. I was just wondering what Ryder Mitchell's story is?"

"Well, actually, Ryder and I grew up together. Our moms were best friends and kind of pushed the friendship on us. I think either way we would have been friends, because we're so much alike. Sometimes I wonder if we aren't secretly related or something, but whatev. Gabe didn't come around until our senior year of high school and Gabe and Ryder became instant friends. They both played on the baseball team and then Gabe introduced himself to me."

"Wow, what a small world, but why are you surprised that Ryder and I are just friends? I'm not really understanding that part."

Sarah didn't get to answer because Jade started talking. "OMG that gorgeous piece of ass is staring at me like hardcore." I looked around the cafeteria and the only person who was staring in this particular direction was Ryder. I couldn't help but notice that a majority of the people at his table were the girls from earlier who'd been listening to him talk after our class together. I also noticed that a bunch of the guys were from the baseball team because they were wearing t-shirts with the school logo on the front.

When he saw me looking at him he smiled and waved. Sarah and Gabe turned to the side and Gabe gave a nod while Sarah flicked him off as a joke. Sarah interrupted Jade's rant. "Darling, he isn't staring at you, he's eye-fucking our girl Iz." Before she could even finish saying my name I started choking.

Jason came around to smack my back. After I was finally able to catch my breath, I looked in Ryder's direction again and saw that he had a scowl on his face.

Maybe he was looking at someone else after all. Jason managed to open my water bottle for me and I took a few sips. Catching my breath, I decided to make my way to my next class. I had definitely had enough excitement for one day.

Before I could open the door, Jason was by my side. "Hey, Iz, hold up a second. Are you okay?" I smiled and nodded my head in the direction of our lunch table. "I'm fine, Jason. Thanks for helping me out back there." He opened the door for me and we walked for a few minutes in silence.

He was just getting ready to ask me something when I felt big, strong arms pick me up from behind. "Hey, sweetheart, you okay?" I smiled because I knew who it was before I even looked behind me. "I'm fine, munchkin, thanks." I found it a little awkward that Ryder didn't let go of me and kept giving Jason these weird looks. "So Jason, what was it you wanted to ask me?" I could tell Jason was trying not to laugh for some reason but he just shrugged and said he would see me later.

Once Jason walked away, Ryder finally let go of me. "What are you doing the rest of the day, sweetheart?"

"I have another class and then I was going to apply for a job. Why?"

"I'm having a party later and I wanted to see if you wanted to come over."

"Oh thanks, Ryder, but I have a lot going on. Maybe some other time?"

He scrunched his eyebrows together and folded his muscled, tattooed arms in front of him. I noticed he started to shift his weight from foot to foot as well and started to act really uncomfortable. "Uh, yeah sure. Sounds good."

I felt bad because he seemed really disappointed. Don't get me wrong; I really wanted to go hang out with him but I had a lot going on today. Plus, I wanted to try to keep my distance from Ryder because I wanted to get over this "crush." I knew there was no way he would ever feel the same way about me. Deep down, I knew that nobody was going to feel that way about me.

***

When my last class ended I went to the library and applied for a job. I was so relieved to see that Ashlynn worked there, too. At least I would know a familiar face if I got the job. Ashlynn told me not to worry about it because it wasn't like people were standing outside the doorways waiting to get a job at the library.

The head librarian came out and took me into the back for my interview. Her name was Meredith Bee. I honestly thought that if there were pictures in the dictionary, hers would be by the definition of a librarian. She was wearing a red and black plaid skirt with a black sweater. Her brown hair was in a bun and reading glasses were falling off the edge of her nose.

She asked me all sorts of questions, but after she found that I loved to read her eyes sparkled. I added that I needed a part-time job, but I would work here anyway because I loved to read. She interrupted me and said, "You're hired! When can you start?" I told her I could start as soon as possible and she told me to start the next day.

For the rest of the day I organized my room and put everything in its rightful place. I stacked all my books on the shelves and put my paintings up on the walls. It seemed like this day was doing a complete one-eighty.

Even though I was exhausted I decided to take my shower that night. Hopefully, I wouldn't get the same results as this morning. I was relieved when I turned on the shower and hot water came pouring down over me. I stood in the shower for a while because my muscles were hurting from moving all my furniture around.

I was too tired to blow-dry my hair so I just toweled it and climbed up on my bed and pulled up my comfy blanket. It only took a couple of minutes before my eyes closed. After I fell asleep I dreamed about dark brown eyes, tattoos, and piercings.

Chapter 3

For the next three weeks I went to my classes and worked at my new job as a librarian's assistant. I also got to know Ashlynn a lot more. She told me she had had the biggest crush on Jason ever since freshman year of college. She was roommates with Jade and the second she'd laid eyes on Jason, that was it. She wanted to take things to the next level but it didn't seem to be in the cards for them. She'd figured she would just be his friend instead. She was also scared to start something because she and Jade were best friends.

Jade told her to just go for it, but Jade and Ashlynn were complete opposites. Jade was more of a wild child and did what she wanted when she wanted. Ashlynn was more reserved, like me. I asked her if she ever regretted not telling Jason and she said, "I would rather be in his life as a friend than not in his life at all." It seemed like a rational decision, but all I could think about were the what ifs.

I also hung out with Ryder a lot. Of course we flirted, but that was like breathing to him. He couldn't help it.

During one of our many conversations I found out that Ryder worked at a local tattoo shop to make extra cash. Music and hanging out with his friends were among his favorite things to do, but tattooing was his passion. He also told me that he'd gotten a full ride to play baseball and that he was double majoring in business and marketing. His ultimate dream was to own a chain of tattoo shops and maybe some clubs in Las Vegas. I wasn't surprised in the least.

He only lived two hours away from school and was really close with his family. He was the baby and had two older sisters, Sadie and Callie. Oh, and I can't forget his love, Rufus the Saint Bernard. Ryder's parents, Todd and Sharon, were high school sweethearts and he said that he really respected his parents and loved them even more because they just wanted their kids to be happy in life.

To live with no regrets.

The way he talked about his family was enlightening but it also saddened me. In that moment I was jealous of Ryder because I couldn't say things like that about my family. *Hell, I didn't even know who my dad was.*

I told him very few details of my childhood, just that I wanted to be an author and before I left this earth I wanted to leave my thumbprint on the world and make a difference somehow. No matter how big or small.

Sarah and I were also becoming fast friends. She told me that she and Ryder tried the whole dating thing in middle school but it was just way too weird. It wasn't until high school that Gabe came into the picture. He moved to Maryland from Arizona and became good friends with .

Sarah was always cheering Ryder on during the baseball games and after they would go get ice cream. One day after a baseball game Gabe had walked up to her and said, "I'm kind of jealous of Ryder right now because I don't have a beautiful girl cheering me on. Feel like changing that for me, beautiful?"

I was surprised when she told me that she hated him at first. I asked Sarah how they became the two people they were today. She smiled and said, "We made a beautiful choice." I asked her what it was and she smiled. "One day you'll know."

Sarah told me that Jade loved being single and was having fun with the guys. It was going to take a very important person for Jade to settle down. She also informed me that Ashlynn had a secret crush on Jason, which I wasn't supposed to repeat to anybody. Too bad I already knew that little bit of information.

I also found out from Sarah that Ryder was a major player. Not only was he an amazeballs baseball player, but he could also get any girl into his bed. He had sex with girls, he never befriended them—until me.

"He had a girlfriend in high school," Sarah started to explain.

I could see she was a little uncomfortable about it. Almost like she wasn't sure if it was her story to tell or not.

Releasing a low breath Sarah said, "Her name was Taylor."

Was?

"They were high school sweethearts and they were really serious. I didn't like her. I thought she was this fake bitch but I think Ryder loved her. Maybe. Anyway, um—" Reaching for her coffee, Sarah took a long sip. "Prom was pretty significant for both Ryder and I. That was the night I fell in love. Ryder on the other hand? It was the night Taylor broke his heart."

"What happened?" I whispered. I almost didn't want to know. I knew that whatever it was had crushed Ryder. More than likely broke his heart.

"She cheated on him," Sarah blurted. They went to this party and I guess Taylor got pretty drunk and had sex with some guy."

"Oh my God," I said. "I can't believe she did that to him."

"That's not even the worst part," Sarah said as she clasped her hands together.

My stomach dropped. "What is?" I whispered. I sort of had a feeling, but I was hoping and praying I was wrong.

"Ryder walked in on them," Sarah let out. "He was crushed. Ended up getting arrested that night and Gabe and I got him out the next day." As Sarah lowered her head I saw her features had changed.

I could tell the Ryder she had known and the one she knew now were two completely different people.

"Anyway, after that he changed. He put up this front and kind of did his own thing, I guess you could say."

"He doesn't seem like that person when he's with me," I blurted. "With me he's this funny, sweet, caring guy.

Lifting her head to look into my eyes, Sarah smiled. "That's how he was before."

I didn't think anything of it until a few weeks later.

***

Sarah and I had decided to get a cup of coffee at Starbucks. We were in a journalism class together and had an assignment due at the end of the week. After getting my Green Tea Frappuccino and Sarah's Vanilla Bean Frappuccino, we decided to sit at the tables and boot up our laptops. I was just getting ready to ask Sarah a question when she interrupted me. "Can I ask you something, Iz?"

"Yeah, Sarah, you can ask me anything, although I might not answer."

"Is there something going on between you and Ryder?"

I took a sip of my delicious creamy beverage. "I wish there was, but no. Why do you ask?"

"It's just I have never seen Ryder look at other girls the way that he looks at you. He never even looked at Taylor like that and they dated throughout high school."

Even hearing her name made my stomach tighten in knots. I couldn't believe that someone had treated Ryder like that. "Yeah, he looks at me like I'm one of the guys, not a girl," I said.

She just gave me a look and said, "Please tell me that you're kidding right now, Izzy. Sweetie, the way he looks at you, it's like you're the exception. His exception." I really found that hard to believe so I just shrugged it off.

After a few seconds' looking at me, she shrugged and we got to work on our project.

***

I was at the library. My sanctuary. I couldn't believe I actually got paid to read books. Okay, technically I get paid to put books away. However, after I finish putting all the books back on the shelves in their proper place, I can read.

I had just clocked out and was getting ready to leave but then I remembered I had to write a paper. I got situated and then decided to check my emails. Among those emails was one from Patty. My stomach instantly tightened and my palms became really sweaty.

Miss Clark,

This is a reminder that this following week is the last week before the $5,000 is due. Please follow the instructions I have attached below.

Sincerely,
Patricia A. Alexander
Financial Aid Office
University of Maryland

I knew this day was coming. I still had to buy books, for right now I was looking off of classmates or the books weren't needed for classes. I think I had maybe $500 and there was no way I could get another extension.

Well, on to Plan B, whatever that was.

I could feel the tears coming so I grabbed my bag, logged off my computer, and made my way out of the library. I was just getting ready to push the doors open when Ryder walked in with a couple of his buddies.

He stopped in his tracks when he saw me. "Hey, guys, I'll catch you later." I felt like a complete moron just standing there looking so helpless.

Ryder pulled my chin up so I would look into his eyes. "Sweetheart, what's wrong?" With those simple words the flood gates opened and I began to cry. He pulled me into his arms, rubbed my back and soothed me. I was starting to calm down and opened my mouth but Ryder cut me off. "I have an idea. We're going to grab a cup of that horrible coffee, go to your room, and talk about this." With that he took my hand in his and pulled me out of the library.

After Ryder paid for the coffees and muffins, we trudged back to my room. We both sat on my bed and there was complete silence for a couple of minutes. I needed a breather and he needed to eat, so he scarfed down the muffins and took half a tuna sandwich out of my mini fridge.

"All right, start spilling," he said while taking a bite out of the sandwich. I thought I had calmed down but the tears just ran down my face as I explained the whole predicament. "I just don't know what I'm going to do. I owe $5,000 to room and board and I have $500 to my name. It's due by the end of this week. I mean, I knew this was coming, so I decided to look at apartments off campus but I don't make enough money for that. And now I'm going to have to move back home and figure something out because I can't live with Cynthia."

Ryder knew my relationship with Cynthia was different but I didn't want to tell him everything that had happened in my life. Some things I had to keep to myself because I couldn't endure seeing the look of pity in people's eyes.

I finally finished ranting and raving and went to the bathroom to wipe my eyes. I grabbed a few more tissues before coming back to my room. After closing the door, I turned around and froze.

I couldn't believe it, I was such an idiot! I'd just ugly cried in front of Ryder and didn't even bother to look at was he was wearing. He was in his baseball uniform. My mouth fell open and, I swear to all of you, I drooled.

"You like what you see, sweetheart?" he said with a smirk.

Dammit, he caught me.

I heard him chuckling and then he swallowed the bite he was chewing. He stood up and started grabbing things and putting them in bags. "All right, I have an idea. Move in with me."

I looked at him like he was crazy. "What are you talking about? I can't move in with you Ryder; that's crazy!"

"Isabelle. I live by myself and have an extra bedroom that I use for storage; it's not that big of a deal. Look, you can live with me as long as you need. Rent free. Save your money for something more important."

"Ryd, I'm going to pay rent or at least for groceries, I'm not a mooch."

He looked at me like I had four heads and said, "Sweetheart, it would be cheaper to pay rent, because you know how much I eat. But you aren't going to pay for that, either. I make enough money to pay for the rent and live comfortably. So pack up your shit and let's go, roomie!"

I was relieved that I would have a place to stay. As a bonus, I found out that Sarah and Gabe lived right down the hall from us. It was Tuesday night though, and I didn't want to move in right this moment. Ryder looked a little disappointed but we agreed that I would move in Friday after our classes were over. Ryder decided to stay over so we could work on our homework together and I got Chinese for the both of us. While we ate we watched some trashy reality television. Eating Chinese food to me is like eating Thanksgiving dinner; it just makes me extremely tired. At some point I fell asleep in Ryder's arms.

I opened my eyes a while later to Ryder pulling back my covers and putting me to bed.

"Where are you going?"

"I'm going home. Sweet dreams, sweetheart."

He kissed me on the forehead and turned off the lights before leaving the room. *Yeah, I was in trouble.*

***

The next morning I was relieved that Sarah and I had our journalism class so I could tell her about everything. I walked into class and saw Sarah was there with two big cups of coffee. Thankfully, she lived off campus so she could stop at Starbucks on her way to our 8 a.m. class.

"Good morning, Iz. You look like you had a good night last night."

I needed a sip of my vanilla latte and smiled because yeah, I did have a good night. No, scratch that, it was amazing.

"All right, spill, Iz. What's with the grin on your face?"

"Well, Ryder came over . . . "

"And what happened?"

I explained everything from the room and board to Ryder offering to let me stay at his place. I spun my cup, looking down at it, and then looked up at Sarah. Her mouth was wide open and she hadn't blinked yet.

I snapped my fingers in front of her face to try and get her attention. "Sarah?"

She blinked her eyes a few times. "I never thought it was possible."

"What?"

"Ryder finding love."

"Sarah, what are you talking about? We're friends, that's all."

"Izzy, honey. You really don't understand. I grew up with Ryder and I thought Taylor had ripped his heart out for good. He was completely different before he met you. He loves you. The question is, do you love him?"

"I don't know. I mean, don't get me wrong, he's gorgeous and really sweet but …"

Did I love him? Yeah, I guess I did. I think what Sarah meant to ask was, "Are you in love with him?" I don't know. I looked up and Sarah was smiling so sweetly at me. I swear she heard all my inner thoughts.

She took a sip of her coffee and thankfully, changed the subject. "What did you think about the assignment?"

I answered her but my heart wasn't in it. I had more important things on my mind like the beautiful man I was going to live with and who I just realized I might be in love with.

I am so royally fucked!

***

I became more and more nervous the closer it came to Friday. This was the exact opposite of how Ryder was feeling. He couldn't wait for me to move in with him and begged me all Wednesday and Thursday to change the date. I decided to stand my ground because I had some things to think about.

I moved into Ryder's apartment on Friday after classes.

When you walked into his apartment there was a kitchen and island to your left with a breakfast bar. To the right was the living room with an L-shaped couch, along with a plasma screen TV. Straight across the living room was a hall leading to the bedrooms. Halfway to the bedrooms was a bathroom to the right and at the end of the hall, two bedrooms faced each other.

Basically, Ryder's apartment screamed, "Bachelor pad!"

After putting everything in its rightful place, I put on some old sweats and grabbed a good book, looking forward to a relaxing night.

"Knock! Knock!" Ryder said while coming into my room. He stopped and just stared at me. I looked up from my book and, oh my Buddha.

Ryder was wearing dark jeans with a red shirt and tennis shoes. His tattoos were on display for all the girls to ogle over but for just a short while I was the only girl ogling.

I was about to collapse from oxygen deprivation because when I looked at Ryder, I forgot normal functions like breathing. Then Ryder ran and jumped on my bed. "Ah, hell no. It's a Friday night, so get your cute little ass up and get ready because we're going out."

"Look, Ryder, I just wanted to relax tonight. It's been a long week."

He stopped jumping and fell on my bed. "Sweetheart, it's a Friday night and we're in college. We're leaving in fifteen minutes. You have the choice of wearing that or something else. It won't matter to me either way because I would prefer you in nothing, but those are your options."

I could feel a blush creeping on so I grabbed my clothes and headed for the bathroom.

I should be in the *Guinness Book of World Records* because I took a shower, freshened up my makeup and hair, and dressed in ten minutes flat! My hair was in waves and I was wearing a tight, knee length, green halter dress with white wedges and clutch. As I made my way into the kitchen I heard Ryder cracking open a beer. He was just about to take a sip when he saw me and his jaw fell open. His eyes bored into me and reached into my soul. I felt jittery and nervous and completely alive all at the same time. His eyes made their way down my body and then back up again, searching mine. He gulped and took a long drag of his beer before shaking his head.

"Nope, not going to happen. Sweetheart, you have to change. Like right now."

Um, was I high as a kite or was Ryder speechless when I walked in?

"Why? What's wrong? I think I look cute," I said, twirling around. When I faced Ryder again he gulped and took a deep breath.

"No, you look gorgeous. Hell, you look gorgeous all the time. Can't you just wear like a brown paper bag or something? No, you know what? You would look gorgeous in that, too. Ugh, fuck! Can you just please, for the love of god, change out of that? I would really like to not end up in jail tonight for beating up fucktards," he said.

I look gorgeous? All the time? In his eyes?

But I'd clearly won this battle because I walked over to the fridge, cracked open a beer and said, "Munchkin, you told me I had fifteen minutes and there are two minutes left, which means I won't have time to change. So how about you just be my bodyguard for the night?"

He chugged his beer and said, "All right, but if I see one asshole look at you the wrong way, we're leaving!"

***

We decided to go to a local bar with a dance floor and music. Luckily, it wasn't too crowded. I was nervous because I wasn't twenty-one but Ryder had it covered and had a fake ID for me. We ordered shots of tequila at the bar. After downing our shots, I ordered a Corona and Ryder got a Bud Light.

I was feeling great after a couple of drinks and really wanted to dance. "Ryder, come dance with me." I didn't give him a chance to think about it because I grabbed his hand and pulled him onto the dance floor. The current song playing was "Superbass" by Nicki Minaj. I was feeling brave from the alcohol and wrapped my arms around his neck and we started to grind into one another. We danced for a couple more songs and then my jam, "Turnin' Me On" by Lil Wayne and Keri Hilson started to play. I immediately turned around and started rubbing my ass up against him. I could feel how much he wanted me through his jeans and I wrapped my arms around his neck. He slowly skimmed my side and I instantly felt goose bumps where his fingers touched me.

I couldn't believe how sensual it was and I slowly turned around in his arms and ran my fingers through his hair. I heard him take a sharp breath and for just a moment we stopped dancing and just stood there, staring at one another. Whatever thought I had of him kissing me vanished the second Jason tapped Ryder on the shoulder. "Mind if I cut in?"

Ryder looked like he was going to combust but he just shook his head and walked back to his seat at the bar. I put my arms around Jason's neck, feeling a little hurt about the way Ryder just walked away.

After a few seconds I asked, "So, Jason, what was it you wanted to ask me?" He put his hands on my hips and slowly pulled me closer. I was facing the bar and could see Ryder's face turning bright red as he strangled the neck of his beer bottle.

What was the matter with him? He was the one who left. Jason and I were just dancing and I wasn't even Ryder's girlfriend. What was I to him? Oh yeah, his roommate.

I tore my gaze from Ryder and turned my attention back to Jason. He looked a little annoyed, but shook it off. "You didn't hear anything I said, did you?"

"Oh, I'm sorry, Jason; the alcohol is just starting to hit me. You mind if we get some air?"

Just as we were walking outside, Ryder pulled me against him. "Okay, we're leaving now."

"Dude! What the hell is your problem? Izzy is fine. We were just getting some air." Jason looked between me and Ryder and didn't know what to do. Hell, I didn't either. Ryder and I were friends, but I could see that Ryder was really pissed off for some reason.

While Jason was really built, I knew that Ryder could break him in half like a twig. I put my hand on Ryder's arm to try and calm him down. "Jason, we're just going to go. I'll see you later?" Jason shrugged his shoulders and before I knew it, Ryder was putting me into his car. He slammed my door shut, got in on his side, and sped down the street.

"Ryder, what the hell is the matter with you? We were just dancing!" Of course Ryder didn't say a damn word the whole ride home.

We had just pulled up to the apartment and I was getting ready to open my car door but Ryder beat me to it. He put me over his shoulder, carried me to my bedroom and slammed the door behind him as he left. I didn't know what to say so I just sat on my bed in complete shock.

A few minutes later Ryder walked in. He looked like he had calmed down a lot and walked over and sat next to me on my bed.

"Look, Isabelle, I know what guys are like and what Jason is after. The way he was looking at you he just wanted one thing. Trust me when I say that Jason doesn't date girls; he fucks them. I knew you were drinking and I just didn't want you to make any mistakes. I'm sorry for the way I acted, but I was just trying to look out for you. To protect you."

I thought I had calmed down but my blood started to boil and I bolted up off the bed.

"You have got some fucking nerve accusing me of that. Ryder, you are the king of sleeping with any girl who's willing to spread her legs for you. And my god, are they willing!"

I wanted to add that I was willing as well. But I don't want to be somebody's *once* but somebody's *forever.*

I could see his head fall and I felt bad for the words that came out of my mouth. After all, he did give me a place to stay rent free and, maybe in his eyes, I was in danger. I took a few deep breaths and bit my lip to avoid saying anything to make the situation worse. I sat by him on the bed and took his hand in mine.

"But Ryder, you really don't have to worry about that kind of stuff with me."

He held on to my hand and turned to face me. "Why don't I have to worry about that with you, sweetheart?"

I thought Ryder was smart enough to read between the lines, but apparently not. Ugh, this was so embarrassing but it would ease his mind and I wouldn't have to deal with any more embarrassing public scenes. So I took a few breaths and said, "I'm a virgin."

Ryder stood up from the bed and burst out laughing. "Shit, you're good. For a second you really had me going there." When I didn't say anything he stopped and looked at me. "Fuck, you're not kidding, are you?" He sat back down on the bed and I shook my head.

"Look, it's not like guys aren't attracted to me or anything. I've had my opportunities, but I haven't really had a lot of choices to make in my life that are just mine. This is the one thing I have and I can make the decision myself. No one else can."

I couldn't understand why I was explaining myself to Ryder, but I felt comfortable with him. He made me feel things that I never felt before. Everything was different between us.

Ryder picked me up and pulled me onto his lap. I thought he was going to make some smart ass comment about my virginity, but he tucked my head under his chin and whispered, "Sweetheart, whoever you choose will be the luckiest bastard known to man."

I couldn't believe what I'd just heard. I took a second to let the words sink in and a smile touched my lips. "Thanks, Ryd, that means a lot."

If it was even possible, Ryder pulled me closer to his chest and then said, "Of course, we could always do the deed right now if you really wanted to."

I slapped him on the chest and giggled. "Thanks, munchkin, I'll take it under advisement. You know I have a ton of suitors available and waiting for me."

He laughed and I could feel the vibration from his chest against me. "Oh, sweetheart. If only." He pushed up from the bed and set me down. "Goodnight, Isabelle. Sweet dreams."

After he left my room, I fell onto my bed and whispered, "If only."

Chapter 4

"Holy fuck, he's gorgeous. I swear, just staring at him I get an orgasm!" Jade was staring past Sarah and me and fanning herself. Sarah just started laughing. "Okay, Jade, who are you talking about now?"

Jade was still fanning herself and looking off in the distance when she said, "Oh, just the sexiest man known to the universe who has every piece of ass groveling at his feet. Except he's staring at Izzy like she's his last meal, Aladdin's three wishes, or the best girl on girl porn video out there. Take your pick. Hell, she could be all three to him."

I laughed at her analogy. *Aladdin's three wishes?* "Jesus, Jade. Could you talk any louder? I don't think everybody heard you."

Jade finally broke her stare. "Oh, come on, Iz. There really isn't anything going on between the two of you? Like seriously, have you not looked at Ryder?"

I didn't look up from doing my homework. Explaining myself was really getting old. "Yes, I most certainly have looked at that gorgeous piece of ass. Normal functions like breathing are hard to do around him. But have you looked at me?"

Nobody said anything for a while so I looked up and they were both staring at me with the dumbest looks on their faces.

Sarah took a long breath and flicked me on the forehead. "Ow, Sarah. What the hell was that for?"

Sarah crossed her arms and looked at me. "Well, I was trying to slap the stupid out of that head of yours. Isabelle Katherine Clark, you are a gorgeous girl, inside and out. I don't know who made you think that you're nothing, but they're completely wrong."

"I'm not saying I'm ugly or anything, but I don't compare to those girls who are always huddled around Ryder. I'm nowhere near his level and never will be. It doesn't even matter if I was on his level or not. Nobody has ever loved me. I don't think anybody ever will. Plain and simple."

Jade dropped her jaw and her gum fell out onto the table. "You really have no idea, do you? Ryder has never looked at or treated a girl the way he has treated you! Sure, he's given girls the best orgasms of their life, but that's all it's been. Hell, he gave me an orgasm just by staring at him. But I didn't think it was possible for Ryder to fall in love, and even if it was, I didn't think I would see the day. It's like witnessing pigs fly or some bullshit like that."

All I could do was laugh. "Jade, you're crazy if you really think that."

Sarah looked behind me and a smile crept onto her face. "Well then, don't turn around." As soon as she said that, it was inevitable that I would turn around. *Come on, people! When somebody tells you not to do something, you are going to do it!*

Ryder and Gabe were walking over to us. Ryder had this huge shit-eating grin on his face and was carrying two cups of coffee and two muffins. After just a few more strides, he handed me a cup and my favorite muffin: blueberry.

"Hey, sweetheart, I thought I'd walk with you to class. You know, since we're in the same Creative Writing class and all?" I was so happy to see him. At times it seemed like we couldn't get enough of one another. While taking a sip of my coffee, I felt Ryder put his arm around me as he sat down and waited for me. I took another sip and then started to put everything in my bag.

I didn't even bother looking in Sarah and Jade's direction because I already knew the stupid ass grins on their faces. We walked out of the cafe and Jade headed back to her apartment. "All right, see you love birds later. Bye Sarah and Gabe."

At that very moment Sarah interrupted, "Well, would you look at that? I forgot that my class was going to be held in the library today. Gabe, isn't your class in the other direction as well? So we'll see you guys later." Ryder smiled and waved. Meanwhile, I gave her the death glare.

Once Sarah and Gabe walked away, Ryder asked me a question. "So you want to explain what Jade was talking about?" He had a shit-eating grin on his face waiting to hear how I was going to get out of answering this question.

"I think you've known her longer than I have. The bitch is crazy, that's all."

He started to laugh. "You're correct on that, but Jade is one of those people who says what's really going on. She doesn't hide her feelings. She just kind of puts it out there and she's never been wrong before."

Oh no, what was I supposed to say? Come on, how to steer clear of this conversation…

"Maybe this time she was wrong. Nobody's right all the time."

I looked over at Ryder and he'd lost that twinkle in his eye. His head fell and he said, "Yeah, you're probably right, I guess."

I felt like all the air had escaped my lungs. I didn't want to be right, but at the same time I was petrified and didn't know what was going on in his head, so I'd just said the first thing that came to mind.

I guess my mom was right about something. I was stupid.

The rest of our walk to class was silent and this time it was most definitely awkward.

The day just seemed to get worse and worse from that point on. Our Creative Writing professor assigned a paper on the topic of love. There was no word length requirement. It could be as short or as long as we wanted, as long as we got our point across … great!

***

Later that night, Ryder and I were both working on our papers for class. We were sitting on the sofa eating pizza. Ryder got up and walked into the kitchen and grabbed two sodas. After making his way back to the couch, he put his papers on the coffee table and got comfortable. "So sweetheart, what do you think?"

I was halfway through writing my paper and decided to take a breather. "About what?" I heard Ryder laughing as he handed me one of the sodas. "What I should wear tomorrow. No silly, I mean about love. What do you think about it?"

I put my paper down and took a sip of soda. Ryder was staring at me, of course. Come to think of it, he was always staring at me. It should bother me and make me feel uncomfortable but it made me feel like he was actually interested in what I had to say. More importantly, it made me feel like he cared about me.

I looked straight into his eyes and took a deep breath.

"I believe in love at first sight. Whether you are in middle school or middle-aged. I believe in long walks on the beach, even though I have never been to a beach, and candle-lit dinners. I believe in his and her towels and sharing the same toothbrush and razor. But I also believe that if I was lucky enough to find that I would run away scared to death and would later kick myself in the ass for it because I lost it. But I also know that I'll never find love and I'm slowly beginning to accept that."

I took a few breaths to calm myself. I felt like a huge weight had been lifted off my shoulders and I didn't realize until that moment that I'd needed to tell someone how I really felt. I have always just kept my thoughts to myself.

Under lock and key.

Hidden away from everyone. Sometimes even from myself.

Ryder broke me from my thoughts. "Wait, you've never been to the beach?"

I looked at him like he was crazy. "Are you serious right now? I just told you something really personal about myself and that's all you took from what I said?"

Shaking his head, he said, "No, I listened to everything you said and it broke my heart. But I'm just surprised that you've never been to the beach. I'll have to change that for you, among other things."

His words made me smile. "Thanks, Ryd. When?"

"Well, I was thinking over the summer. You know? So I could see you in a hot bikini." And then the bastard winked at me, which made me laugh.

"Okay, enough about me. What about you, Ryder? Have you ever been in love?" I thought I knew the answer to that question, but Ryder surprised me yet again. Without taking his eyes off me, he took a sip of soda and said, "Yes."

I wondered who it was. I remembered Sarah telling me all about Taylor and thought maybe it was her. Whoever the girl was, she was lucky. Not because it was Ryder, although that was a plus in and of itself, but because somebody actually loved her.

I tore my eyes away from Ryder and took another sip of my soda. I couldn't bear to see the look in his eyes when he talked about this girl because for a split second I wished that girl was me. "What was she like?" He shrugged and took a couple of steady breaths. It seemed like it was a hard subject for him and I was getting ready to ask a different question when he opened his mouth.

"She's a spitfire and she has no idea how beautiful she is. It always looks like she has something on her mind. It seems like she has the world on her shoulders and I just wish that I could take away all of her pain. I know she's been through a lot in her life, but she never lets it get to her. I can tell that somebody has really beaten her down and broken her spirit. It just makes me want to beat the living shit out of that person for making her feel the way she does. While she's the smartest person I know, she can also be so blind, because I thought I'd gotten my feelings across, but I'm either not trying hard enough or she just thinks very little of herself. I want to be the one who helps her. Takes care of her. I know we could be something really great. The only question is whether she's willing to take that leap of faith with me. I'm just waiting for her to open her eyes and see what's standing right in front of her."

The whole time he was talking I was playing with a loose string on the end of my pillow. I could feel his eyes on me and I looked up and saw that I was right. He was looking at me with such sincerity.

Like he was trying to send a message that only I could receive, but I didn't understand what it was.

The only thing I could think about was how I wished that girl was me, but nobody would ever love me the way Ryder described that girl on his mind. So I did what I do best and shrugged my shoulders.

"Ah, unrequited love? Well, all I can say is, that girl is really lucky and I hope that maybe someday I'm lucky enough to have somebody think that way about me. Maybe. And Ryder, sometimes we girls just need the guy to be straightforward with us. No games." He let out a low laugh and then looked at me.

"Yeah, I guess you do."

I felt like a topic change was in order, enough of sharing my feelings for one night. I also couldn't take the sad puppy dog look in Ryd's eyes for much longer. "Ryder, can I ask you a question?"

He was now twiddling his thumbs and looking down at his lap. "Yeah, sweetheart, you know you can ask me anything."

"I want a tattoo and I want you to design it for me. Will you do that?"

He stopped what he was doing and looked at me with a glimmer in his eyes. "Yeah, I can do that. Is there something in particular you're looking for or do I get free rein?" That was the way I liked Ryder; happy and carefree.

"You have free rein but nothing stupid like a cheeseburger." He started to ask me a question when I interrupted him and said, "No, you cannot put your name on me."

He started to laugh. "Damn, how'd you know I wanted to make you mine?"

I knew Ryder was joking around but a little part of me wished that he was being serious. But that wasn't my reality. We sat for a few moments in silence and then Ryder grabbed his soda and finished it off. "All right, well, I'm all done with my paper and now I have to design a pretty bad ass tattoo for my girl. So I'll see you tomorrow." He got up off the couch, bent down in front of me and kissed me on the forehead. "Sweet dreams, sweetheart." Then he walked into his bedroom, closed the door, and turned on the stereo.

I took a few minutes to let everything sink in. I took a few more sips of my soda and made my way to the fridge. I opened it and pulled out a bottle of white wine and then opened the freezer and pulled out a pint of cookie dough ice cream.

Yeah, nothing like eating some ice cream to mend my heart and drinking wine to help me forget about it. For now at least.

Chapter 5

October seemed to fly right by. Ryder and I were getting even closer, as if that were possible. I thought we would start to get on each other's nerves when I moved in with him, but it was the opposite effect, actually. We were always hanging out with one another. When I moved in I honestly didn't think Ryder was going to be around all that much because of the rumors of him going out to parties and getting girls in bed, but he became a homebody like me.

We would eat dinner together, watch movies, and play card games. It actually kind of surprised me. The first day I met him he invited me to a party at his place but he hadn't thrown a party here yet. It didn't really bother me because I was enjoying my alone time with Ryder. I swear I learned something new about him every single day. Like how he was deathly afraid of clowns or how he absolutely loved country music. Kenny Chesney and the Eli Young Band were among his favorites.

Sarah and Jade still didn't believe me when I said nothing was going on and we were just friends, but they let it go.

Jade was still being Jade, which was having fun and not having a care in the world. Ashlynn started dating a guy from her Chemistry class, Derrick Miles. While Derrick was cute, there was just something odd about him that I couldn't put my finger on. Ryder didn't like him either, and told me to stay away from him, saying he didn't get a good vibe from the guy.

Then all of a sudden Jason was seeing this girl named Christy Allen who he said he'd met at a party. She seemed nice, but she was a little ditzy. Sarah told me that Christy was her roommate freshman year, although she didn't know a lot about her. Christy was always going out and often times spending the night somewhere else.

What surprised me the most was that Jason would act really weird whenever Ashlynn and Derrick were around. It didn't matter if Christy was there or not. Jason would stiffen and glare daggers at Derrick. He tried to push it off as if he felt Ashlynn was a sister but Ryder and I both knew something was going on in Jason's head, or heart.

Sarah and Gabe were still going strong. There are some couples who are really nauseating, but Sarah and Gabe were so cute. They complemented each other really well. I always questioned true love, but when you looked at Sarah and Gabe, true love was no longer a question, it was an answer.

Sarah reminded me so much of Jade, with a bit of a filter. Whenever Sarah would talk I loved to watch Gabe. The way he looked at her made my heart melt. He looked at her with such affection and I knew what they had was real. That maybe it really was out there and that I could maybe have it. That maybe it was a possibility.

I could feel something was changing between Sarah and Gabe because Gabe was starting to act nervous and became really jittery whenever he was around Sarah. I thought maybe something had happened between them, but Sarah seemed like her same old self. I was starting to get nervous. When I couldn't take it anymore, I asked Ryder about it one night. He told me that Gabe was going to propose over Thanksgiving break. He told me not to tell anyone and that he was the only one who knew. I was so excited for them and I just wanted to see the ring. Ryder told me that he'd helped Gabe design it and that started to make me think about the tattoo that Ryder was still designing for me.

I had only known everybody for three months, but it felt like I finally had a family. Since Sarah and Gabe only lived across the hall, we would have family dinners once a week. We also went to the movies and did normal things couples do.

Wait, where did that come from?

***

I was sitting in the living room drinking a glass of wine and reading a book when Ryder came home from work. He took his shoes off and pulled off his jacket. "Honey, I'm home." We always made it a ritual when he came home. I would run into his arms and give him a kiss on the cheek, but tonight it was different.

I put my glass of wine down and looked at Ryder and smiled. I started to run into his arms and he lifted me up and held me against him. I don't know if it was instinct, but I wrapped my legs around his waist and my arms around his neck. The room was so quiet; it felt like time stood still forever. My eyes bulged out of my head and my heart beat so fast. I could hear Ryder breathing just as hard as I was.

I was getting ready to say, "Welcome home," but I didn't get to say anything because he kissed me. The second his lips touched mine I felt like I was electrocuted and brought back to life. Before this moment, it felt like I wasn't really living. I finally understood what all the love songs and sappy romance novels were about. His lips gave me the answer.

He was staring at me, asking a question that only I could answer. Ryder started to pull back, but I grabbed his head and crushed his mouth to mine. I heard him moan and he opened his mouth, patiently waiting for me to open mine in acceptance. The second our tongues touched I felt wet between my legs. Ryder pulled me even closer and I felt his growing erection right at my crotch.

One of his arms wrapped around my waist and the other was at the back of my head, trying to deepen the kiss. I started to sigh, which in turn only made Ryder groan louder. His groans made me feel animalistic and I wanted to devour him. Make him mine.

We kissed for a few more seconds and all I wanted at that moment was for him to carry me back to his room and finish the job. No scratch that. Not job, because people work at jobs because they have to. With Ryder I wanted to.

I wanted him.

In that instant Ryder started to put me down. I wanted to grab his hand and pull him back to his room. If he wasn't going to take the initiative, then I was.

The second my feet touched the floor, I felt like I was going to fall over. My legs were weak like jelly. I couldn't hold myself up. I don't know if I was reading way too much into it, but Ryder grabbed ahold of me and never let go. I felt like he saved me and that maybe I could start to open up my heart. That maybe with Ryder I could be saved and that everything I'd been dealt in my life might have been worth it.

My eyes slowly fluttered open and I saw Ryder's pupils were dilated. He was looking at me like he wanted to rip my clothes off. I kind of wished he would. I was about to ask him why he didn't but he shook his head. I took that as a sign that the kiss didn't mean as much to him as it did to me. Not even close.

"Damn, sweetheart, that was fucking amazing. I think I'm going to work every day from now on if I get a kiss like that when I come home."

I tried to laugh it off. "Hey now, come on, munchkin. I believe you kissed me first."

A slow smile crept onto his beautiful face and then it disappeared. "Yeah, I did, and I'm so happy you ended it."

The second he said that I pushed out of his arms and walked away. I never took my eyes off his. I felt like I'd been punched in the gut and the wind was knocked out of me. I thought I heard my heart breaking, but maybe that was just the deep breaths I was trying to control. I couldn't believe I'd thought Ryder could save me or want me. Or that anyone would want me.

I walked into the living room, got the glass of wine and my book, and started to make my way toward my room. I was getting ready to close the door but Ryder blocked the door with his foot.

"Sweetheart, what's wrong?"

I gulped down the rest of my wine as I made my way over to the bed. "Nothing's wrong, Ryder. Nothing at all. Everything is just the way it should be."

Ryder clearly wasn't buying my act. "Then tell me why you look like I just told you Santa Claus isn't real for the first time?"

Here it was. Now or never. "Am I not a good kisser?"

"What the hell are you talking about, Isabelle? You're fucking amazing. I'm just glad you stopped."

I couldn't believe I was going to ask the question, but I had to hear the answer even though I already knew what the answer was going to be. "Why? Why are you glad I stopped if I'm *fucking amazing,* as you put it?"

"Jesus. Is that what this is about? Because I said I was glad you stopped?"

When I didn't say anything and just stared at him, he continued.

"Sweetheart, I'm glad you stopped because I was about to drag off all of your clothes and sink right into you. That's why I'm glad you stopped, because I wouldn't have been able to."

"What makes you think I wanted you to stop, Ryder? Did you ever think that maybe I wanted you just as badly as you want me?"

Ryder's eyes bulged out of his head and he let out a deep breath.

"Sweetheart, please. Don't say things like that. I already want to kick myself in the ass right now as it is. The words that are coming out of your beautiful, bruised lips are just killing me. Destroying me, even. They're eating me up from the inside out."

"Why not? For once I'm telling you how I feel. What I want. What I choose. And I choose you." The second the words left my lips I didn't know what to do. The truth was finally out there, that I wanted Ryder Mitchell.

Ryder walked back and forth in my room for a few seconds and took a deep breath. It looked like he was debating something with himself, but the second I saw him shake his head I knew I wasn't going to like the answer. "Sweetheart, the reason I'm glad you stopped is because I wouldn't have been able to."

My blood boiled and I lost it. I had put my empty glass down on my nightstand but I was still holding onto my book like a shield, trying to keep myself safe from his words. I threw my book at the wall and just started screaming at him. "Dammit, Ryder, I know! You already told me your goddamn fucking excuse!"

"Fuck, Iz! It's not a fucking excuse! It's the goddamn truth! I have wanted you ever since I ran into you and I looked into your beautiful brown eyes! You took my breath away, but I knew something that beautiful didn't deserve to be in the same place as me, let alone be with someone like me. You deserve so much more than me, Isabelle Katherine.

"I don't even know if there's someone out there who comes close to what you deserve. You deserve someone who's going to love you forever and who's waiting for you like you're waiting for them. You deserve respect, and God, if they could give you the world, they should. You deserve to be cherished and at the top of their priorities, but with you I don't know how any man could have any other priorities. Fuck, I don't even know how many girls I've been inside, let alone their names. I'll be damned if I let someone like that near you … even if that person is me."

I thought my heart had broken earlier, but it shattered into a million and one pieces with every word that came out of his mouth, his confession. That he wasn't good enough for me. At that moment I wished I had more wine to drink, to make myself numb and forget about all of this, but I didn't. And a part of me didn't want to forget, because while his words destroyed me, they gave me hope. Hope that maybe Ryder and I could work out and start something. I'm not sure what that something was but I knew I wanted it with Ryder. I was done thinking with my head and thinking about the what if's and what could be's. I decided to take a chance and risk everything and for once, I decided to think with my heart.

I untangled myself from the bed and stood up. Ryder was up against the wall in the corner of my bedroom with his arms up covering his face. I couldn't believe that this beautiful man was in so much pain when I was around him. I'd had no idea and it nearly killed me.

I walked over to him and put my hands on his arms. I felt him flinch underneath my touch, but I dragged his arms down to uncover his face and what I saw completely destroyed me. Tears were pouring from his eyes and I didn't know what to do. I ended up doing the only thing I could think of.

I put a hand on each side of his face and cradled him. His eyes were still closed when I leaned up on my tiptoes and kissed him. To me, that kiss symbolized my saving him. I wanted to take away all of his pain. I thought he was going to push me away and walk out of the room, but he pulled me close and spun us around.

My back slammed into the wall and his tongue was in my mouth before I could even comprehend the slight pain in my back. His hands roamed up and down my body and his mouth was ravenous. I felt like he wanted crawl up inside of me and never come out. I thought I knew Ryder, but in that instant it all came crashing down on me in big waves that this beautiful man standing in front of me devouring me inside and out and completely consuming me was even more damaged than I was.

Eventually, Ryder pulled away and leaned his forehead up against mine. With such tenderness and compassion he started to wipe the tears away from my face. "Sweetheart, it's okay. Please don't cry. I'm sorry I told you. I've wanted to tell you, but I knew it would destroy our friendship. I'm so sorry for everything. I'm just going to be in my room when you want to talk." He let go of me, opened my door, and walked out.

I thought the kiss that we just shared was him giving in and allowing me to be with him, but instead, the kiss was more of a goodbye, and it answered so many of my questions. I fell down the wall and curled up into a ball. This was all happening so fast. I wiped the rest of the tears away from my face, but it didn't do me any good because they just kept coming. I tried to settle myself as best as I could and took a few calming breaths. I needed to get my bearings together in order to talk to Ryder.

A few minutes later I stood up and walked over to his room. I knocked a few times, but there was no answer so I just walked right in. Ryder was sitting on his bed with his head between his hands looking down at the floor. He didn't move when I knelt in front of him. I wanted to move his head so he would look at me when I told him my confession, but his stare would shatter me, body and soul.

"The first time I saw you I thought you were physically beautiful. As I have gotten to know who you are as a person, I've learned that your physical beauty comes nowhere near in comparison with how beautiful your heart and mind are. I spent my entire life with Cynthia telling me I'm not worth it, that I'll never be wanted, cherished, loved. I thought that what she was telling me was true because if my mom couldn't even love me, why would anybody else? But that all changed when I met you. You changed everything for me.

You have shown me that people do care about my well-being and that there are good people out there. What I'm saying, Ryder, is that everybody has a past and we do things we might later regret. I can't change mine and even if I wanted to, I wouldn't, because if I had done anything differently I might not be sitting here in front of you confessing my feelings. We might not have even met and I wouldn't be able to live with that. I already told you that I chose you and I still choose you. I might regret things I say or do, but I will never regret choosing you. I will always choose you. The question now is, what do you want? Who do you want? Who do you choose?"

Ryder looked up from the floor and put his hands on my face and swiped his finger across my lips. It looked like he was having an inner battle with himself and every second that went by, my heart beat erratically quickened.

"Motherfuck. I don't deserve you, Isabelle, but for as long as you'll have me, I'm yours. Only yours."

I didn't think my lips could take the loneliness anymore. I was about to kiss him, but he leaned in to me and kissed me with such tenderness that I became weak in the knees. It was a good thing I was kneeling in front of him, because I would have fallen straight on my ass. His kisses never seemed to get old and I didn't think they ever would. They took my breath away and showed me there was so much more out there.

After kissing me, he looked at me with such thoughtfulness in his eyes. "So, sweetheart, where do we go from here?"

"I don't care. It doesn't even matter where we go from here as long as I'm with you."

A smile touched his lips for the first time since we kissed at the front door. "I couldn't have said it better even if I tried."

***

"Shut the front door, you bitch!" Jade was jumping up and down and squealing. Sarah had this mega-watt smile on her face and her eyes were twinkling. "So what, are you guys like a couple or something? Oh my god, this is fucking crazy!"

I stood up and started to pull Jade back down to her seat. "Jade, please calm down. We're in the library, for goodness sake."

The second Jade's ass touched the seat, she jumped back up and started to leave the library. "Jade, where do you think you're going?"

Jade stopped dead in her tracks and turned around. "Um, what does it look like I'm doing? I've never seen pigs fly. I'm just going outside to see what they look like." She turned and walked out of the library.

"Cheese and rice, it's not that crazy that we're dating. Is it, Sarah?"

Sarah was still smiling at me and I hadn't seen her blink in a while, so I waved my hand in front of her face. "Sarah, are you okay? Are you broken or something? Do I need to reboot you?"

Sarah laughed and slapped my hand away. "Oh, you smartass, I'm fine. I'm just shocked, is all, and extremely happy. My two best friends are dating. I just can't wait to help you pick out your wedding gown and throw you the best bachelorette party ever!"

The second I heard the word *wedding* my stomach dropped and I became speechless.

Sarah waved a hand in front of my face like what she had just said was not that big of a deal. "Oh sweetie, calm down. I'm just kidding around, but honestly, I could see it happening. Don't worry and don't you dare let it get to you, okay? Matter of fact, how about you just forget I said anything?"

"Um, yeah. O—okay." Like that would happen.

By the time I was done with my internal freak out, Jade came back in the room and fell down into her seat. "Well, I missed them. Thanks a lot, Iz. So how amazeballs is he at kissing? Did you instantly orgasm?"

"Oh my gosh, Jade, you really are crazy! All I'll tell you is that his lips are amazing and his hands are …"

"What about my hands, sweetheart?"

My heart sped up and I started to turn around. Ryder was looking down at me with a huge smile on his face and those damn dimples were making a sexy ass appearance. "Um, exactly how much did you hear? And who said I was talking about you, munchkin?"

He started to laugh and bent down and kissed me on the lips. I thought it was going to be a simple peck but he put one of his hands behind my head to deepen the kiss. Then his tongue was in my mouth swirling around with mine and his other hand was on my hips, holding me still. I heard sighs from behind me but I was way too mesmerized by Ryder's lips. I was hypnotized. I started to put my hands up around his neck to play with his wavy hair but he broke away. His lips moved up into a devilish grin and his eyes sparkled. "So who were you talking about, sweetheart?"

Ryder knew he had me right where he wanted me. I decided to go with the truth and see what he had to say about that. "You. Only you."

His smile got even bigger and I swear I saw fireworks go off in his eyes. "So, you ready to leave? I'm really hungry. How about some dinner?"

"Um yea—" I didn't get to finish my sentence because Ryder pulled me up over his shoulders and turned to walk away.

Before we made our way out of the library, I heard Gabe yelling, "'Atta boy!"

Sarah laughed and Jade yelled, "So that's what the kids are calling it these days? Dinner? Well, I hope you two have some really spicy, hot, dirty dinner!" then she winked at us.

Chapter 6

I was sitting in the living room doing some homework when Ryder came up behind me and sat down on the sofa. I could tell that his eyes were on mine and I smiled. I looked over at him. He handed me a glass of wine while he took a sip from his bottle of beer.

I took the wine from him and took a good healthy sip. "Thanks, munchkin." I leaned over and kissed him on the lips. I heard him moan which made me giggle and also got me really excited, a.k.a. *horny as fuck.* I couldn't believe in a million years I was the one getting Ryder to make sounds like that.

Ryder stood up and set his beer on the coffee table then took my wine and set it down next to his beer. He then sat back down and looked at me. "Why are you always staring at me, Ryder?"

He shrugged his shoulders like it was a no-brainer, almost as if I should know his answer to my question already. "Because you're gorgeous.

Beautiful. Sexy. Hell, those words don't even come close to describing you. It's just that I can never get enough of you. Every time I look at you, I see a different emotion come across your face or a new freckle I hadn't noticed before. Why? Does it bother you?" I actually thought about it for a few seconds and then shook my head. "You know what? I thought maybe it would bother me, but it doesn't. It actually makes me feel cherished and special."

He wrapped an arm around me to pull me closer and kissed me on the forehead. "You are very special to me, Isabelle. Very special indeed." His words made me want him and before I knew it, I was straddling him and crushing my mouth to his. I twined my fingers through his hair and pulled back just a little so his head would fall back onto the couch. I wanted to take control and deepen the kiss. He happily obliged and wrapped his arms around my back. I could hear him grunting. I sighed and it just made me want him even more than I already did. I didn't want to leave his mouth but I started to kiss down his neck and made my way up to his earlobes to bite down on them.

My lips were getting lonely so I kissed him on the lips again and bit his lower lip. The second I did that his bulging erection pushed into my groin. *Yup, I would definitely have to keep that bit of information at the forefront of my mind for later.*

Then it was my turn. Ryder suckled and nibbled his way down my throat to my collarbone. He started suckling at a soft spot along my jaw. My instincts kicked in and I started rubbing up against his groin. *Oh, I like that feeling!*

I could feel there was a tension building up inside of me and I just wanted to set it free. I needed to find a release. My release. I started grinding into him harder, which gave him all the motivation he needed. He started sucking and nipping at my neck harder and his hands moved down my back to grab and pinch my ass. I knew I was getting close and the second Ryder sucked on my earlobe, I completely lost it. I came, and man, did I come hard.

"Oh God. OH GOD, RYDER! RYDER! "

I heard Ryder grunt again and then he became still. Ryder was slowly kissing my neck and kissed me once on the lips while I was still panting and trying to catch my breath.

"Holy shit, sweetheart! The was a—fucking—mazing!"

"Holy shitballs, yeah, it was." I started to blush. *Oh god, I cannot believe I just did that. With Ryder.*

"Um, sweetheart, why are you blushing?"

"Uh… uh, no reason."

"Sweetheart?"

"Ye…yeah?"

"Was that the first time you've had an orgasm?"

"… Um, yeah?"

"Holy shit, if that's what it's like with you just rubbing up against my dick for the first time, I can only imagine what it's going to be like being inside you."

"Ryder?"

"Yeah, sweetheart?"

"Did you? Y—you know?"

He started to chuckle.

I looked at him because I was really confused.

Nudging me to get off him, Ryder nodded his head towards the bathroom. "I'll just be a few minutes."

"I could help," I offered.

"No," he said as he shook his head.

"No?" I asked.

Sitting back down on the couch, Ryder wrapped his strong arms around me and pulled me to his side. "Isabelle, babe. Calm down, okay?"

"Okay," I whispered.

After pulling me onto his lap, Ryder demanded, "Look at me."

Lifting my head up, I looked at Ryder and released a low breath.

"Isabelle—" Sucking in a breath, he said, "The reason I said no is because I enjoyed watching you get off. That's what this was about. Not for you to jerk me off. Okay?"

"Okay," I answered hesitantly.

"Isabelle, we will, okay? Don't worry," Ryder assured me. "Just not this time."

"But when?" I asked.

"When we have time to get used to one another's bodies." Ryder smirked at me. Ryder started to nudge me off of him to get up and go to the bathroom then said, "Oh I wanted to ask you something first before I forgot. What are you doing for Thanksgiving break?" I hadn't really thought about that. God knows I wasn't going back home to have Thanksgiving with Cynthia. I hadn't heard from her since I'd left for school in August. I didn't really have any family back home and the only friends I had were the ones I had made here. Maybe I would just have a quiet break and read a lot of books. I had started a list of books that I wanted to read at the beginning of the year. I was kind of disappointed that I couldn't read as much as I wanted to because I was so bombarded with all of my classes. "I don't know. Why?"

"Well, I had an idea I wanted to run by you. I wanted to see if you would come home with me for Thanksgiving break. You know? Meet my family and everything?"

"Are you sure? I mean, is it too soon in our relationship to do that?"

"Sweetheart, I was going to ask you to come home with me anyway and meet my family. But now I don't have to introduce you as my roommate. I get to introduce you as my girl."

My stomach fluttered from the butterflies and my heart skipped a beat.

"What are you smiling about, sweetheart?"

"Just the way you said 'my girl' and how lucky I feel to be the girl. Your girl."

"That's just one of the many things I love about you, sweetheart." He kissed me on the lips and then made his way to his room.

The second he closed the door I let out the breath I didn't realize I was holding. I thought I was going to have a heart attack because the last words Ryder said to me kept playing over and over in my head, *That's just one of the many things I love about you, sweetheart.*

This was moving way too fast, way too soon, and it was scaring the living shit out of me.

***

"I mean, Ashlynn, I don't know what to do. I thought it was going to be amazing dating Ryder. I mean besides the fact that he's drop dead gorgeous, his heart and his mind are just beautiful. But it's all just moving way too fast. He invited me home to meet his family for Thanksgiving and I thought the idea was amazing. But earlier in the day, Sarah was talking about bachelorette parties and weddings, so I was already scared. Then I said something that had Ryder saying, and I quote, "That's just one of the many things I love about you, sweetheart." Okay, I'm officially done bitching to you. I just needed to word vomit and let someone know how I feel about the whole relationship." I was in between stacking books on shelves and complaining to Ashlynn.

"Well, at least the guy you want wants you back."

I finished putting the book I was holding in my hands on the shelf and turned to Ashlynn. "Okay, what the hell is going on with you and Jason? And besides, I thought you were dating Derrick?"

Ashlynn was in the middle of handing me another book when she started to laugh out loud. "I have to tell you something top secret and you have to promise me that you won't tell anyone. I mean anyone. As in this is a life or death situation. Do you understand exactly what I'm saying, Izzy?"

"Ashlynn you are really freaking me out right now. What the hell is going on?"

Ashlynn put the book down on the cart and dragged me into the breakroom. After looking around and closing the door, she pushed me over to the couches that were set up against the wall. "Okay, here it goes. Technically, I'm not actually dating Derrick."

"What do you mean, technically? You either are or you aren't, so which one is it?"

"Derrick is gay and some people have been giving him a hard time on the football field. They've been making jokes about how they never see him with pussy and he wouldn't know where the vagina was even if he had a map. Since we're lab partners and we've gotten to know one another, he felt really close to me and told me all of that one night while I was complaining about Jason and how he was 'hanging out' with Christy. So Derrick had a brilliant idea that we would help out one another by *dating*. He gets the guys on the football team to lay off and I get to make Jason jealous, or attempt to. But it didn't work."

I was completely speechless for a few minutes and Ashlynn snapped her fingers in front of my face. Then it all came rushing back to me. "Holy fucking shit! I totally did not see that coming. Ashlynn, I thought Derrick was like a creep and crazy or something. I had no idea that you guys planned this. That's fucking crazy!"

"I know, right? I was completely fine with helping Derrick out but what I don't understand is that even though Jason's dating Christy, whenever he sees Derrick touch me, he looks like he's going to kill him. I thought maybe he would break up with Christy and confess his undying love for me, but that's just my stupid, crazy imagination, and of course, all of those books I've been reading. Maybe he really does see me as his sister."

Ashlynn started to slump over and I wrapped my arms around her to hug her. "Ash, I don't understand exactly what his problem is, but I can tell you that that boy really likes you. In fact, he's crazy about you. Maybe he's just scared. I mean after all, you and Jade are like best friends and all. Maybe he doesn't want to ruin a friendship if you guys break up. Or maybe he's just like you… he'd rather be in your entire life as a friend than just be in your life for a short while as a boyfriend."

I turned to give Ash a kiss on the cheek when I saw a tear fall from her eyes and I quickly wiped it away. "Ugh, Iz, you're right. But you know what? I've felt like this since freshman year of college and I'm tired of trying and failing. It's his turn, so I'll continue to help Derrick out. But in the meantime, I'm just over it. Maybe, just maybe, Jason will man up."

It was her decision to make and maybe she was right. She's had these feelings for a long time and maybe Jason was just one of those people who wants what he can't have. Or maybe he's finally realizing what he's had right in front of him for the past three years.

"I'm so tired of talking about my drama. So what's this about you and Ryder? Is it really scaring you that much?"

"Yeah, it's actually scaring the shit out of me. I don't know, I mean in one day Sarah is talking about weddings, Ryder is inviting me to his family's house for Thanksgiving break, and then he says that he loves something about me. It is just *a lot* to take in."

"If it really bothers you, I would talk to him about it, but this is a side of Ryder nobody has ever seen before. It just means that you're really special to him and that's saying something when he's a senior in college and he hasn't had a girlfriend since high school. You know?"

"Yeah, I guess. Don't get me wrong. Ryder is amazing and I thank God every day that I'm with him, but again it's just moving way too fast. I feel like he's going to propose over Thanksgiving break and I'll be pregnant by Christmas."

"Oh sweetie, calm down. You'll be fine at his family's house. Plus Sarah lives right next door to him and Gabe lives on the next street over, so there'll be no worries at all. Okay? Just try to enjoy yourself."

"Thanks, Ash. I really needed that pep talk. I really appreciate you listening to my complaining and all."

"Anytime, Iz, anytime. And remember what happened in this room stays in this room. Okay?"

I took my hand and ran it across my lips. "Your secret is safe with me, Ash."

***

"Sweetheart, are you all packed up for break?" Ryder walked into my room and sat on my bed while I finished packing my suitcase.

"You know what, I don't think this is a good idea. What if your family doesn't like me? God forbid, what if Rufus doesn't like me? I think I'll just stay here. I can celebrate Thanksgiving with some Chinese food and wine—lots and lots of wine. So it won't be all that bad. Plus I'll have some good books to read, so you won't have to worry about me. I'll be fine."

Ryder pulled me onto his lap and wrapped his arms around my waist. "Sweetheart, you have to stop worrying about things like that. You're my girl and you're really important to me. As for my parents, they will automatically love you. Rufus loves just about anyone. As long as you have a treat with you, you're golden. You have to watch out for Sadie and Callie, though. They'll tell you all of these crazy ass stories about me when I was younger, but you have to remember, sweetheart, that I was young and stupid. Plus they were all before I met you."

I started to calm down and kissed him on the cheek. "Thanks, Ryd, I really needed that." I started to get up from his lap but he pulled me back down and I felt his erection pushing up against his jeans.

"That's really all I'm going to get, sweetheart? A kiss on the cheek?" Of course, he had to give me that sexy ass smile and those damn dimples made an appearance. I got up from his lap and he started to protest, but before he could say anything I quickly yanked his shirt over his head. I then pushed him back onto the bed. He was laughing a little but a look of seriousness took over his facial features the second I straddled him.

"Um, sweetheart, what exactly are you doing?"

In the sexiest voice I could manage without trembling, I said, "What's it look like, Ryder? I'm going to kiss you."

I started by kissing and licking at his belly button and made my way up to his nipples. *Oh dear fuck, I'm going to come right damn now. His nipples are fucking pierced.*

I looked at them and my mouth dropped open.

Ryder lifted his head from the pillow and looked down at me. "Is everything okay? I was starting to really enjoy tha—"

"Your nipples are pierced."

"Yeah? Do you not like them? I could always take them out if you want. It's not that big of a deal."

He started to place his hands on a nipple and I screamed, "NO!"

Ryder immediately stopped what he was doing and looked at me questioningly. "Ryder, you have no idea how much I want you. Then I see your damn nipples are pierced and I want you even more right damn now! Don't you dare even think about taking those piercings out." I grabbed ahold of his hands and pushed them up over his head and bent my head down and swiped my tongue along one of his nipple rings.

"Shit, Iz. You're going to kill me." I just smiled against his nipple ring and moved on to the other one.

Ding! Ding! DING! One point for this girl right here.

While I felt like I could stay at his nipple rings forever and ever and ever, I moved up to his neck and sucked as hard as I could. I heard Ryder start to laugh and felt the vibration against my body. "Damn, sweetheart. What do you think you're doing?" He bent his head so he was looking at me.

I shrugged my shoulders a tiny bit and tilted my head to the side. "Why, whatever do you mean, Ryder? I'm just making sure everybody knows that you belong to me. That you're mine and I'm yours."

In an instant Ryder's hands were at my waist and he flipped me onto my back. I was breathing hard and I heard Ryder panting. "Say it again, Isabelle."

"What?" My heart was beating out of my chest. What was going on in that head of his?

"Say it."

I finally understood what he was telling me to do. "You're mine and I'm yours."

"Yes, sweetheart. Say it again."

With as much conviction as possible I said, "You're mine and I'm yours." I thought he was going to kiss me on the lips but he swiped his tongue along my neck and before I could moan out in appreciation, I felt him sucking on my neck. I tried to push him off me but that just wasn't going to work out in my favor. He was at least a foot taller than me and boy, was he built. He probably had a good hundred pounds on me so it was a lost cause. I could feel his lips press up into a smile and heard his laughter. "Sweetheart, that attempt you just made was downright pathetic. You know that, right?"

"Did you ever think that maybe I was playing around? That I enjoyed the feel of your body up against mine, the weight of your body? Maybe I was just trying to move you up a tad bit so you would devour my mouth."

And with that he crushed his mouth to mine. I greedily opened his mouth with my tongue and while one of my hands was roaming up and down his back, the other was flicking each nipple ring. God, those nipple rings would be the death of me. Could it get any better? I mean, really?

After a few minutes Ryder jumped up off me and started to walk out.

"Now where do you think you're going, Ryd? I wasn't finished with you just yet!"

He ducked his head back in. "Oh well, you know I just had this hot girl underneath me making me exceptionally hard. So I have to go take a cold shower to calm down." I wanted to finish him off but then the bastard fucking winked at me like he could read my mind and left my room.

When the door was completely closed, I fell back on my bed. "Fuck me." I didn't think I said it too loud but I heard Ryder from the bathroom yelling, "All in good time, sweetheart. Haven't you ever heard patience is a virtue?"

"And haven't you ever heard of using your hand? I'm pretty sure you don't want to use that the rest of your life! Oh by the way, how's that cold shower working out for you in there?"

When I didn't hear him say anything, I started to giggle. I'd finally shut that boy up, so I was pretty damn proud of myself. I was beginning to stand up when I looked at the doorway. Ryder was standing in the doorway, dripping wet with just a towel on. His ripped muscles, abs, and that V were on display and the V was disappearing beneath his towel. It kind of reminded me of an arrow. Almost as if it was pointing at his dick and there was a halo and bright lights signaling that it was exactly what I wanted. I swear I could hear angels singing and see Heaven's gates opening up. My mouth fell open and I didn't move.

"Do you like what you see, sweetheart? You know a fly or something might go in that beautiful mouth of yours. Then what would you do?" The whole time the bastard was smirking at me.

I instantly regained my bearings. "Well, I would rather have the something over the fly any day. If you know what I mean?" I scanned his entire body, stopped on his crotch, then made my way back up to his eyes. I winked at him.

Beat that, you sexy bastard!

Now it was Ryder's turn to stop dead in his tracks with his mouth open. I could see him trying to readjust himself and then he hit my wall. "Goddamn! Well, another cold shower for me, myself, and I."

Finally! I beat that sexy ass boy of mine!

I got up from the bed and began to finish my packing when there was a knock at the door. I walked into the living room and opened the door to find Gabe standing there.

"Hey, Gabe. What's up?"

"Hey, Iz. I just needed to ask Ryder something. Is he around?"

I smiled to myself thinking about where he was and why. "Um, yeah, he's actually taking a shower right now. He shouldn't be much longer if you wanted to come in and wait for him?"

"Thanks, Iz. There's actually something I wanted to talk to you about, too. Between us, if you don't mind."

I was so excited. I thought maybe he was going to ask me my opinion on how to propose to Sarah. You know, since Ryder spilled the beans on that secret and all. Gabe sat at the breakfast bar and I got two waters out of the fridge and handed one to him. "So what's up, Gabe? What'd you want to talk about?"

Gabe took a sip of his water and then set it down. "It's actually about Ryder." The second he said that my heart stopped and I couldn't breathe. Oh no. What happened? What did he do?

I guess Gabe could see the scared look on my face because he said, "Iz, it's nothing like what you're probably thinking, so calm down. Just take a few deep breaths in and out. I just wanted to talk to you about Ryder. He's my best friend and I don't want to see him get hurt." I walked over to Gabe and sat down on a barstool as he kept going.

"It's just that you know about Taylor and that crushed him. After they broke up, he just kind of lost it. I mean, he thought he was in love with Taylor and I could have seen him proposing to her, but she smashed his heart into a million pieces. I honestly didn't think he would ever get over it. You know about Ryder's past and how he just used girls. Well, anyway, what I'm trying to say is that from the moment he met you, he's changed. He's different now because of you. All I'm saying is that

I don't want to see you break his heart. He's been through a lot and he's dealt with a lot. I thought he was in love with Taylor and he went into a depression after they broke up. So I can only imagine what would happen if anything happened between the two of you. I know you would never cheat on him because I see the way you look at him, but I'm just looking out for Ryder and letting you know. If something ever happened between the two of you it would destroy him."

Holy shit! This is moving way too fast. Too fast! Too FAST!

I blinked a few times and took a sip of water before I said anything to Gabe. "Look, Gabe, we just started dating. I really care about Ryder and his well-being and I would never do anything to hurt him. You just have to trust me on that. If anybody were to get hurt, it would more than likely be me."

Gabe looked at me and nodded his head in understanding. "I think you guys are honestly perfect for one another. I doubt that you would ever hurt him or that he would ever hurt you, for that matter. I just wanted to let you know what I thought."

"What you thought about what?" Ryder walked into the kitchen, wrapped his arms around my waist, and looked at Gabe. Gabe took another sip of his water and punched Ryder on the side of the arm. "Oh, how ugly I think you are. You know, nothing personal. I just don't understand how a beautiful girl like Iz here chose an ugly ass like yourself."

Ryder turned me around on the barstool and looked me straight in the eyes and started shaking his head. "I have no idea, either. But I'll take it as long as I'm lucky to have it." Then he kissed me. I started to get lost in the kiss when I heard Gabe get off his barstool and walk over to the door. "Well, I'll see you guys later tonight, then?"

Ryder looked up at Gabe and said, "Actually, my family was just going to have dinner at our house and we were all going to hang out. You guys are definitely welcome to come over, but if not, maybe later in the week?"

Gabe nodded and opened the front door. "Yeah, sounds cool, dude. You guys have a safe drive." I was still staring at Ryder but then remembered that Gabe wanted to talk to Ryder. I jumped up off the barstool and turned to Gabe. "Wait. Gabe, didn't you need to talk to Ryder?"

Gabe was halfway out the door when he turned around and smiled. "You know what? I'll just catch up with him later. See you guys." After he closed the door, Ryder hugged me to him and I wrapped my arms around his waist. He kissed me on the top of the head and then looked at me. "You ready, sweetheart?"

I smiled and said, "Yeah." But for how much? That I wasn't sure.

Ryder pulled away and smiled down at me. "Awesome. I'll go get the bags and then we can get going. How about you just go sit in the car and wait for me, okay?" I nodded my head. "Sounds good, Ryd."

Before I could even finish the sentence, Ryder was already on his way back to the rooms. I walked over to the front door and started to open it, when realization smacked me right across the face.

What was I going to do?

Chapter 7

"Sweetheart, we're here. It's time to wake up." Ryder nudged me again and I started to open my eyes, noticing how bright it was outside. I closed my eyes again and started to yawn. I couldn't believe how tired I was, but damn, that hour nap felt so good. I slowly opened my eyes again and wiped them. I yawned again, then looked up at Ryder, who was smiling down at me.

"Oh, Ryder, I'm sorry I fell asleep. I guess I was just really tired." I sat up in my seat and pulled down the visor to check and make sure my mascara wasn't running down my face or that I didn't have eye crusties in the corners, or worse, dried spit running down my mouth.

Oh thank god, I looked somewhat normal.

I let out a big puff of air and pulled my eyelash curler out of my purse to recurl my eyelashes. Sure, Ryder had come into my room in the morning to wake me up. He'd seen the bird's nest that I call hair hanging down my shoulders, the dried toothpaste on the center of my mouth and the little burps I make after drinking soda or beer. But I was his girlfriend now and girlfriends don't sweat, burp, fart, or poop. We look perfect all the time. And if we did poop, it would be glitter or butterflies to make it more feminine.

After I put the visor back up, I saw Ryder was staring at me with a huge smile on his face. I started to laugh at him. The way he was always staring made me think I'd cast a spell on him. Was I a witch or something? Could I cast spells? God, if I could, I would definitely help out the poor guy I saw the first day of class. I would totally use my powers for good. Pure, honest good.

I put my hands on his shoulders and started to shake him. "Ryder, why are you staring at me?" He smiled again and those damn dimples were up front and center, just instigating the shit out of me. God, what I wouldn't give to be at our apartment alone for thirty minutes. No, an hour. I started to blush and Ryder had a smirk on his face.

"What exactly is going through that beautiful head of yours, sweetheart?"

I tried to cool off a bit before I answered, "Oh, if you only knew." Ryder winked at me and stepped back as I got out of the car. I turned around to close the door and when I turned back, Ryder had his hands on my hips pushing me up against the car. I wrapped my arms and legs around him.

Before I could say anything, Ryder kissed me and his tongue was swirling around with mine. I instantly took ahold of the back of his head and ran my fingers through his soft brown hair. I heard him moan and my stomach went crazy. It completely turned me on when he made noises like that because of me, and it only made me more determined.

I started to put my hands under his shirt, and just like that, he put me on the ground and stepped away from me. I felt like someone stole my air. I looked down at my hands and then looked at Ryder. He was breathing really heavily. He put his hands in his front pockets and looked me in the eyes. "Will that hold you for a short while, sweetheart?" He had no idea how much he turned me on. And it actually started to piss me off, because like every other girl out there, I started having an argument with myself in my head. I was thinking I wasn't good enough. That there was someone else better out there. That he could do so much better than me. That I wasn't worth it. And then of course those thoughts only led my mind to places that I didn't want to go, my mother.

You are nothing. You will never be anything.

I shook my head and swiped my fingers through my hair. I was about to tell Ryder that maybe this whole weekend was a mistake. However, when I looked up into his eyes, my mind quickly changed. In his eyes was pure hunger. I bit my lip and put my hands on my hips. His eyes narrowed in on my mouth and I let go of my bottom lip and ran my tongue across where my teeth just were. I could see Ryder breathing even heavier than before and then he glanced up into my eyes. It looked like he was about to blow right then and there and that only made me even more determined.

I shook my head back and forth, never taking my eyes off his. "Not even close, Ryder. I don't think you really have any clue just how much I want you." A smile started to creep onto his face and within a second, Ryder was standing over me. I thought he was going to kiss me, long and hard. It made me think of another part of his anatomy. But what he did was so much better. He grabbed my hand and put it onto his crotch.

Holy fuckballs!

He looked down at my mouth and saw that it'd fallen open and laughed. "I think I have a pretty good idea, sweetheart. In fact, a very good idea." I was still stunned speechless when Ryder kissed the corner of my mouth and swatted my behind. "Now let's get all of the bags out of the trunk and go meet my family. Okay?"

I couldn't form words, so I just nodded, which only made Ryder laugh at me more. He kissed my forehead and said, "All right, let's go." I walked to the back of the car with him and grabbed my bag. After closing the trunk, we started to walk over to his house and I stopped in my tracks.

This wasn't just a house, it was a home. There were cars in the driveway and a basketball hoop standing by the garage. There were also toys scattered all over the yard, ranging from pom-poms to bicycles. There were wildflowers planted everywhere and the house looked like it came out of a fairytale book. There were a few weeping willows to give them their space from the neighbors and a pool in the backyard. The house reminded me of a cottage, a very huge cottage.

Ryder broke me from my thoughts and placed a hand on my lower back. "Ready?"

I gulped a few times, shook my head, and looked at him. "Yeah?" But for how much I couldn't say.

We started walking up the driveway and I tripped over a huge bone. Ryder dropped his bags and caught me. I had my arms wrapped around his neck and he dipped me and winked at me. Ryder was about to bring me back up, when his family came out. His mom laughed and said, "Well, don't just stare at her. Kiss her, Ryder."

I started to blush and Ryder winked at me. "I have to listen to my mom." Suddenly his lips were on mine. I got so carried away with the kiss that I slipped my tongue in his mouth and heard him moan. I giggled and he brought me back up. I started to grab my bag when he turned me around to hug me and said, "Behave, sweetheart. You're really tempting me right now."

I laughed and turned to him. "Well, it's about damn time, munchkin." I winked at him, grabbed my suitcase, and headed over to meet his family.

I put my hand out to introduce myself to his mom and dad when I saw that they had a weird look on their faces. I turned to look at Ryder and saw that he wasn't standing next to me. I turned around and he was back where I left him. I laughed and winked at him again.

Point for me!

He shook his head and joined the three of us. "Mom, Dad. This is Isabelle Clark." Again I put my hand out and said, "It's nice to meet you both, Mr. and Mrs. Mitchell." They looked between themselves and started to giggle. His mom pulled me into a hug and I dropped my suitcase. "Oh honey, please. Call me Sharon and this here is Todd. Okay?" After she let go of me, Todd gave me a quick hug.

Ryder put his arm around me and I said, "It's nice to meet you, Sharon and Todd. Thanks so much for having me for Thanksgiving. I really appreciate it." I could feel Ryder's eyes and looked at him and smiled. I looked back at Todd and Sharon and saw that Sharon's eyes were twinkling with excitement. "Oh honey, it's not a problem at all. We're really pleased you accepted the offer. I just feel bad that you're not with your family for Thanksgiving."

That instantly took the smile off my face and I didn't know what to say. At that moment, Ryder said, "How about we go on inside? I want to show Isabelle where she's staying and she's a little exhausted from the drive here."

Sharon smiled again and said, "Yes, absolutely." She grabbed my hand and started to drag me into the house. Todd laughed and patted Ryder on the back. Before Sharon and I were inside, I heard Todd say, "Well done. You found yourself a good one, I can tell." I wish I'd heard what Ryder said but the door had already closed behind us.

I took a second to take off my shoes and then just stared. The house was so beautiful. It was an open floor plan like our apartment. The kitchen was huge with every gadget you could think of. It had pots and pans hanging from the wall and cookies were spread out all over the island. Damn, the house smelled amazing, like sugar and spice … and everything nice.

The living room was right across from the kitchen. It had big comfy couches facing a fireplace; above the fireplace was a huge flat screen television. Through a corridor was the dining room with a brown table and eight chairs. There was fine china in glass cabinets and I saw senior pictures of Ryder and his two sisters, Sadie and Callie. In the corner of the living room was a shrine filled with pictures of the kids at all different ages and trophies from baseball, cheerleading, and soccer.

I turned to look at Sharon and told her how beautiful I thought the house was and how comfortable I felt being in it. Her exact response was, "I'm an interior decorator, so it should be gorgeous. I was going for homey because just like you said, I want people to feel comfortable. I want them to put their feet up and relax. But I almost killed Ryder the one time he came home from baseball practice when he was younger and put his muddy shoes all over the sofa. He said, 'But Mom, you said you wanted people to put their feet up and relax.' He said it with such sincerity I just laughed and gave him a kiss on the forehead. That little boy could do no wrong; he just melted my heart. Of course Todd was angry because he had to scrub and scrub to get all the mud off the couch. But by the time it wasn't visible, I decided to redecorate the whole first level of the house."

I started to laugh but then I heard scuffling sounds coming our way. I saw a huge shadow and then a bear of a dog appeared in front of us. He looked like he could eat me for a snack. Sharon saw my eyes get huge and chuckled. She pulled a treat out of her pocket and said, "Give this to Rufus and he'll be your best friend."

I was still nervous but I felt a little safer when Sharon leaned down next to me to see Rufus. I held the cookie in the palm of my hand. As Rufus walked towards us, my heart beat faster and faster. He stopped right in front of me and I saw slobber coming from his mouth. Before I knew it he took the cookie out of my hand and scarfed it down. He looked at me again and I thought he was going to kill me but he licked my hand for extra crumbs. I started to giggle because his whiskers really tickled my palm.

Sharon sat and smiled. "He likes you." Rufus got closer to me and licked the side of my face, which only made me giggle more.

I kissed him on the top of the head and started petting his fur. Without turning around to look at Sharon I said, "I like him, too. He's really sweet and so cute and cuddly."

I kissed him on the head and heard Sharon say, "I wasn't talking about Rufus." I turned around to look at Sharon and saw tears forming in her eyes. I didn't know what to do and I was so relieved when I heard the door open and in walked Ryder and Todd.

Ryder winked at me, which made me smile. Just being in his presence made me feel safe. Todd walked up to put an arm around Sharon and then saw she was tearing up. "Oh darling, what are you crying about now?" Todd looked at me and smiled.

"You'll have to excuse my wife. She cries at just about everything, so don't mind her."

I just smiled and stood up to join Ryder. Rufus nudged my leg and I looked back at him. I patted him on the head one last time. Ryder picked up my bag and I followed him up the stairs to the bedrooms. I thought I'd be in the guest room but I walked into a room filled with baseball everything. It looked like somebody literally threw up the sport. There were bats hanging on the walls, trophies in a display, and signed autographs from Jered Weaver of the Los Angeles Angels, Matt Kemp of the Los Angeles Dodgers, and Justin Verlander of the Detroit Tigers.

Ryder explained that since his dad is a pilot, he befriends a lot of celebrities and gets tickets to a bunch of baseball games from all over the place. I smiled and sat down on his king size bed. I could have fallen asleep right then because it was so soft and comfortable. Ryder sat down next to me and took my hand in his. I looked at him out of the corner of my eye and said, "So this is where all the magic happens. This is where you bring all the ladies?"

I heard Ryder laugh and then he got serious. He was tracing circles on my wrist when he said, "Nope." I looked into his eyes. "Not even Taylor?" He never stopped tracing the circles when he said, "Not even Taylor. You're the first." His confession made my heart melt and I felt warm all over.

I smiled. I don't think I've ever smiled as much as I have when I'm with Ryder. There's just something about him. I looked around the room again and stood up and turned to face him. "So where's my room?" Ryder looked around like he was contemplating something and then looked back at me. "It's right here."

I felt my heart stop and I started to freak out. "Ryder, I can't stay here. This is your parents' home and I don't want to disrespect them. I mean, I just met them and I want to make a good first impression." Ryder stood up and put his hands on my shoulders. "Sweetheart, relax. We're adults and they said it was fine. We don't have a spare room and if you really feel that uncomfortable about it, then I can just sleep downstairs on one of the couches. Okay?"

I looked into his eyes. As much as I wanted to cuddle up next to him at night and fall asleep in his arms, I knew him sleeping on the couch was the best idea. "Okay. Can you sleep on the couch? I would just feel more comfortable with that."

Ryder laughed and kissed me on the forehead. "I was kind of hoping you wouldn't say that, but yes, sweetheart. Anything for you." He kissed me on the forehead again and then released me. "So are you hungry or anything? What would you like to do?"

At that exact moment I yawned and Ryder laughed. "All right, I'll let you sleep. I'm going to go downstairs and hang out with my family. Just come down when you wake up. Okay, sweetheart?"

I nodded and as he was leaving my room, I heard a bunch of screaming and then, "OMG! Where is she?" Ryder turned back and laughed. "I think that nap is going to have to wait because one of my sisters is here, and by the squeal I think it's Callie."

Oh boy. No turning back now.

Chapter 8

Ryder came over and gave me a hug. "Are you ready, sweetheart?"

I grumbled into his chest and mumbled, "Do I really have a choice?" I could feel the vibrations of his laughter coming from his chest.

"I'm going to say no to that." He gave me another quick squeeze and put me at arm's length. "I'm ready whenever you are, sweetheart."

I loosened up and took a deep breath, trying to psych myself up. "Bring it on."

Ryder took my hand in his and we left his room. We were at the landing when I heard, "So what's she like?".

Then I heard his mom say, "She's beautiful and you can tell she really likes him. I don't know, but I just have a feeling."

His sister squealed again and said, "A feeling about what?"

Right then we walked into the living room and Ryder said, "That I'm the luckiest guy out there."

Everybody said "Awww," and then there were three pairs of eyes on me. My face reddened and I waved with the only hand I had available since the other one was crushing Ryder's because I was so damn nervous.

Ryder let go of my hand to pick his sister up and twirl her around. "Oh my god, munchkin, I missed you so much! Did you add some new ink to your arms?" My heart warmed because she called him munchkin just like I did.

Ryder put her down and kissed her on the cheek. "Yeah, sis, just a few here or there. But Isabelle over here is letting me design a tattoo for her."

"When is this tattoo going to be done? It better not cover up my entire body," I said. Ryder leaned into me. His warm breath was against my ear and I had instant goose bumps which made me shake.

He stiffened but then shook it off and said, "Soon, sweetheart. Very soon." He took a few steps back and his sister came over to me.

Her eyes got huge and she had a big smile on her face when she introduced herself. "Hi, I'm Callie." She was so pretty. Like Ryder, she had big brown eyes and brown hair, but that's where the comparisons stopped. She was really tiny and petite like Sharon. I could tell just by how she talked that she was a cheerleader. I put my hand out to shake hers, but she giggled and turned to Ryder. "Munchkin, she's adorable."

She turned back to me and wrapped me in her arms. What was with these people giving hugs? It was as if Ryder could read my mind because he put an arm around me and said, "We're a hugging type of family."

Sharon broke the silence. "Come on, everybody, let's sit down in the living room. I've made sandwiches and there are a ton of cookies, so you guys better eat them all up." We walked into the living room and sat down on the couches. Ryder pulled me closer and put an arm around me. "Mom makes the best peanut butter cookies ever. You definitely have to try one or five."

Sharon handed out drinks, and after everybody got comfortable, Callie asked, "So how'd you two meet?"

Ryder laughed and said, "Well, I kind of ran into her. Literally." Callie, Sharon, and Todd laughed.

I was looking at Ryder, smiling at the memory, when I heard, "So how'd you guys end up living together?" I couldn't tell who said it; Sharon or Callie, because I was too caught up in checking Ryder out. Ryder laughed and looked at me like he knew what I was doing. I blushed and looked at his family, who were waiting for an answer.

I told them how my financial aid didn't cover all of my room and board and how Ryder offered me his extra room. Callie laughed and said, "That sounds like Ryder. He's always trying to save things." Sharon and Todd laughed with her but my stomach dropped.

Was that what Ryder was doing? Trying to save me? Did he even like me?

I felt hurt and broke Ryder's grip on me and picked up the glass of iced water to take a sip. I sat back down on the couch but I made a little bit of room between me and Ryder. He glanced at me and he looked really hurt. Good, I was hurt, too. I didn't need saving and I wasn't a project for him to do.

I looked back to the rest of his family and saw that Callie, Sharon, and Todd were laughing. They had clearly missed everything. Sharon was holding a family photo album and walked over to show me a bunch of pictures of Ryder as a little boy. She told me how he would take in stray animals and how he would help wounded birds. As he got older he volunteered at homeless shelters and visited retirement homes. I looked at the pictures and smiled, but then I remembered that he was trying to save me and my smile fell.

After seeing a few more pictures, we went out to the kitchen to load up on dinner. Sharon didn't feel like cooking since tomorrow was Thanksgiving, so there was a huge array of sandwiches, chips and salsa, and cans of soda and a pitcher of iced tea. Returning to the living room, we watched a movie while we ate. I started to nod off halfway through the movie and excused myself to go upstairs. I was halfway up the stairs when I heard Callie say, "I really like her. There's just something about her."

I walked into Ryder's room and was about to close the door when Ryder pushed it open. I just huffed out a breath and sat down on the bed. Ryder was still standing in the doorway with his arms crossed against his chest. "You want to explain to me what that was all about downstairs?"

I looked down at my hands. "I'm not a project and I'm not a charity case. I don't need saving." Ryder kicked off the door and came towards me. He knelt down in front of me and put a hand on each side of my face and forced me to look at him. "I know you're not a project or a charity case. I know you don't need saving …"

I could tell he wanted to say something else. "But …"

He took a breath and said, "But I can tell that somebody has crushed your spirit and I'm just trying to show you in any way I can that I want to prove them wrong. I want to prove to you that not everybody is like that. I just wish that you trusted me enough to let me in. That's all I'm asking and I can see how much it has affected you. I just want you to know that whenever you're ready, I'll be there. Waiting."

I didn't know what to do, so I did what I do best. I started to cry. Ryder pulled away from me. I thought he was going to leave me. Finally he would realize that I'm not good enough for him. But he did the exact opposite. He picked me and laid me down on the bed. I was facing him when he lay down next to me and pulled me closer. I grabbed ahold of him and just cried into his shirt. He rubbed my back and spoke calming words the entire time.

I don't remember falling asleep but I felt the bed dip and then Ryder started to walk away. I sat up and asked him where he was going.

"I'm just going to get the couch ready, but I'll be back to say good night." I smiled and nodded. After he closed the door, I went over to my bag and changed into a pair of cotton shorts and a tank top. There was a bathroom in Ryder's room, so I washed my face and brushed my teeth. After turning off all the lights I went back over to the bed and wrapped myself in the soft blue blanket.

I was just about to fall asleep when I heard a knock as the door opened. I sat up and saw Ryder standing there in just a pair of boxer shorts. He smiled at me and walked over to my side of the bed. He gave me a quick kiss on the cheek. He said, "Goodnight sweetheart," and was just about to close the door.

I sat up. "Wait. Ryder?"

Ryder looked back at me curiously.

"Will you stay with me? Please?"

Ryder smiled and nodded. He stepped back inside and closed the door behind him. He turned back to face me and for a few seconds he just looked at me. He walked back over to the bed and laid down facing me. I turned on my side and for a while we just looked at one another in complete silence. The only sounds were us breathing in and out.

He started to rub up and down my arm and I got instant goose bumps from his touch. I didn't know how to say it, so I just blurted it out. "My mom."

He stopped rubbing my arm. "What, sweetheart?"

I looked into his eyes and explained everything. "My mom, Cynthia. When she found out she was pregnant with me, my dad left. For as long as I can remember, she has been putting me down. Saying I was a mistake. I wasn't worth it. I was nothing. Nobody would ever love me. She didn't, so why would anyone else?" I could feel tears running down my face. I was so ashamed that I was telling

Ryder this but then I looked up and I saw tears coming down his face, too.

He pulled me closer. "Sweetheart, your mom is fucking stupid. If she really thinks those things, then she's crazy. You're an amazing person, both inside and out, and don't you ever, I mean ever, forget it. Please, promise me that."

He kissed me on the lips and that's exactly what I'd needed. I wrapped my arms around him and deepened the kiss. I heard him moan and I knew it was over. I wrapped a leg around him to pull him closer. This is what I needed. I needed to just forget everything.

Ryder pulled back. "Sweetheart, we can't." His voice broke at the end and I knew it wouldn't take long to convince him that this is exactly what I needed. I kissed him again. "Ryder, please. We don't have to have sex, but I just need you close to me. Please, I'm begging you."

Ryder let out a breath he was holding and then he was on top of me. He kissed me with such ferocity that I lost it. I wrapped my legs around him to pull him even closer and rubbed my arms up and down his muscled back. He moved a hand up my shirt and then his hand was caressing my nipple. He was pinching and pulling. God, it felt amazing. He pulled back from me and sat back on his knees. I propped myself on my elbows and looked at him. "Ryder?"

He looked at me and a tear fell down his face. I sat up and wiped it away. "Ryder, what's wrong?"

Ryder looked at me and just started sobbing. "I just, I just want to help you forget. But you're going to have to bear with me. Okay, sweetheart?" I nodded and sat there waiting for him to continue. He put his hands at the bottom of my tank top and started to pull it over my head. I got goose bumps and started to tremble.

This was the first time a man had seen me topless. Ryder looked at me and sighed. "You're beautiful. So damn beautiful." He leaned into me and kissed me as he pushed me back onto the bed. One of his hands cupped my face while the other pinched and twisted each of my nipples. I started to moan into his mouth and then his hand lowered to my shorts. I could feel his hand shaking with nervousness.

He put his forehead to mine and opened his eyes to look at me. "Sweetheart?"

I was too nervous and too excited all at the same time to see where this was going—I just nodded yes. Ryder sat back on his knees again and pulled my shorts and panties off. He dropped my clothing onto the floor by the bed, never taking his eyes off me.

I was lying completely naked in front of this beautiful man. I thought the first time being naked in front of someone I would try to cover up, but not with Ryder. Even though I was so vulnerable, I felt safe with him. Completely and utterly safe.

He leaned back into me and kissed my stomach and then swirled his tongue in and out of my belly button. I moaned in appreciation and wrapped my hands in his hair, pulling him closer. He kissed his way up and left a trail of kisses behind. He stopped at one nipple and looked into my eyes. I pulled my lower lip into my mouth, waiting in anticipation. The second he saw that, his eyes turned lustful.

Without taking his eyes off me, he pulled my nipple into his mouth and started sucking. He pinched and pulled at the other and I was going wild. It was crazy what his mouth could do to me. I thought I was going to finish right there, but then I heard a loud pop and he went to my other nipple. I moaned a little bit louder and I heard Ryder laugh. He moved up so he was looking me in the eyes. He wiped a stray hair from my face and said, "Sweetheart, as much as I want to hear you scream my name when you come, you're going to have to keep it down. Okay?"

I had no words, so again I just nodded. He kissed me on the forehead and then his lips were on mine and his tongue was in my mouth. One of his hands was on my nipple and the other started moving down my body. The second his finger touched me there I thought it was my undoing. Not once did his mouth leave mine. He grazed his hand up my inner thigh and I pulled my legs as far apart as they would go and wrapped them around his body.

I couldn't believe he was going to touch me down there. I felt one of his fingers enter me and then I heard him groan. Like really loud. "Fuck, sweetheart, you're so wet." I just giggled and then bit down on his lower lip and sucked it into my mouth. After letting go, I said, "As much as I want to hear you groan, you're going to have to keep it down, munchkin." He looked back at me and an evil, sexy grin came across his face. "If that's how you want to play, sweetheart." He kissed me once more on the lips and started to move down my body.

Before I could even comprehend what he was doing, I felt his tongue lick me.

HOLY FUCKING SHIT! OH GOD!

I moaned and I heard him laughing. He looked at me and put a finger to his lips. "Shhh, sweetheart." I bit down as hard as I could on my lower lip and watched him. His tongue went wild on me, sucking and licking. I could feel my body beginning to tremble and then he slid a finger inside me. He moved it in and out and God, I was so close.

His mouth never left me and then he slipped a second finger inside me. I could feel the beginnings of my orgasm and then his other hand moved up my body and began to pull and twist one of my nipples. He pinched, licked, and went in and out once more and then I finished. I thought I was going to cry because the orgasm just kept coming and coming. I was panting. Drops of sweat fell against my face when Ryder came crawling up the bed and winked at me. I pulled him to me and kissed him.

My taste was still on him and it just made me wet all over again. I licked up and down his face and sucked his lower lip into my mouth. We kissed each other a few more times and then Ryder fell onto his back, pulling me with him. One of my arms and a leg were wrapped around him and his fingers were playing with my hair.

I couldn't believe that we'd just done that and I started to giggle. Ryder bent his head to look at me with a smirk on his face. "Something funny, sweetheart?"

I looked up at him and smiled. "I now understand what all the fuss is about."

Ryder pulled me closer and kissed my forehead. "Well, I'm glad. Now close your eyes, sweetheart."

My eyes were closing and my breathing was becoming even, but before I completely fell asleep, I swear I heard Ryder say, "I love you, sweetheart."

Chapter 9

Waking up in Ryder's arms was like nothing I had ever experienced before. He made me feel safe. Then I noticed that I was still naked and Ryder only had on boxers, but a part of me didn't care. I should have felt embarrassed, but it just seemed natural for us. My head was resting in the crook of his arm and my arm was across his middle. I could tell from the way his stomach was moving up and down that he was still asleep.

Ever so slowly, I moved my arm and started to draw circles on his abs with my fingers. I started to move out from his arm. I sat up and looked down at him. His hair was all over the place and my God— he looked sexy when he was awake but he was beautiful when he was sleeping.

He looked so peaceful and content and a part of me wondered if it was because of me but I felt like I would only be disappointed in the answer.

You are nothing. You will never amount to anything.

I didn't want to spoil the great mood I was in, so I placed a leg on either side of him and started to kiss his neck. I licked and sucked and nibbled. I looked up into his face and the bastard was still sleeping. I started to wonder how far I could actually go to get him to wake up and then a mischievous smile came across my face.

I scooted to the top of his boxers and started to pull them down just enough for his package to make an appearance. Because it was morning, he was hard. I placed a hand at the base and licked my lips and then moved my head down. I was a little nervous and my heart was beating out of my chest because I had never done this before. I was starting to question whether or not I should be doing this. I knew that Ryder, unlike me, had experience.

I took a deep breath, licked my lips again, and kissed the head. I heard him groan. I looked up but he was still sleeping, so I opened my mouth wide and sucked him into my mouth. One hand was at the base moving up and down and the other was massaging his balls. I was moving my head up and down really slowly and then I heard Ryder moan, "Holy shit, sweetheart." Even hearing Ryder moaning made me wet. I giggled and just hearing him moan gave me all the motivation that I needed, so I took him into my mouth as far as I could go. When I felt him at the back of my throat, I pulled back. All the while I was still moving my hand up and down and using the other to massage his balls.

He moved my hair aside, wanting to get the best view he could. I heard him breathing heavily in and out and then I felt him get bigger in my mouth.

Ryder said, "Sweetheart, you better move because I'm going to come."

I felt him trying to pull me up but I took him in as far as I could without choking. I lightly pulled his balls and then felt him coming in my mouth. I had heard that it was salty, but Ryder tasted sweet. I swallowed and then lifted my head and licked my lips, never taking my eyes off his. I saw him lick his lips and then he said, "My turn." Before I knew it, I was lying on my back and Ryder was making me feel like the only girl in the world.

***

After getting ready, Ryder and I made our way downstairs. His mom was in the kitchen making Thanksgiving dinner. Ryder's dad and Callie were in the living room watching football. Ryder pulled me in that direction but I let go of his hand and made my way into the kitchen to help his mom.

Growing up, there was never much in the refrigerator. While I wasn't able to cook often, I loved the idea of cooking. I loved watching cooking shows and I always bought cookbooks because one day I hoped to try all of the recipes. It was on my bucket list, as pathetic as that sounds. I even took a bunch of cooking classes in high school because I loved it that much. I could sauté and chop and bake like nobody's business.

I noticed Sharon was making the stuffing, so I walked up beside her and asked what she needed help with. I could see that she could really use it. She was getting frustrated, so when I asked, she smiled. She asked me to make the cranberry sauce and told me that the recipe was in their family recipe book. I'd always wanted to try making homemade cranberry sauce because Cynthia and I always had the shit out of the can.

I pulled out the cranberries, orange juice, and cinnamon and read through the directions. It seemed simple enough but I knew the flavors would be anything but simple. A few minutes later everything was added into the pot and it was boiling on the stove. I added sliced green apples, and before you knew it, I was pouring the sauce into a chilled bowl and placing it in the freezer to get cold for dinner.

That's how the rest of the afternoon went. I helped Sharon out in the kitchen making pumpkin pie, sweet potato casserole, homemade biscuits, and a corn casserole while Ryder, Callie, and Todd watched the game.

By the time dinner was ready, everyone was starving. Sharon had made the table absolutely breathtaking. An autumn tablecloth was on the dining table with orange plates and wine glasses and the food was splayed out all across the table. It honestly reminded me of a table assortment that Sandra Lee would do. It was that gorgeous.

After holding hands and saying grace, Todd carved the turkey and Sharon poured wine in each of our wine glasses. After dishing out all of the plates, we ate for a few minutes just enjoying the flavors and the company that surrounded us. At my first bite of turkey, I moaned with enjoyment and I heard Ryder take in a deep breath and then I felt his hand on my upper thigh. Next thing I knew, Ryder accidentally dropped his fork on the floor and when he bent over whispered, "Sweetheart, you better stop making noises like that before I carry you upstairs."

I could feel my face getting red but I couldn't help it. The turkey just melted in my mouth and the gravy was delicious. Not to mention that I had kicked that cranberry sauce's ass.

Callie broke the silence. "So, Ryd, how long are you and Isabelle staying with us? I thought maybe Isabelle and I could go shopping and get to know one another." I smiled on the outside but internally I was freaking out. I felt comfortable around his family, but I didn't want to get really comfortable in case something happened between Ryder and myself and I never saw them again. But then I heard Ryder say, "Oh, we're actually leaving tomorrow."

Well, I guess that's settled then. I'd thought we were having a great time but maybe Ryder just didn't want me getting too comfortable around his family, either. I guess I couldn't hide my emotions very well because he leaned over and kissed me on the cheek. Then he whispered in my ear, "Isabelle, I can't go much longer without hearing you screaming my name. Plus, I have a surprise for you."

I blushed and smiled simultaneously and then I heard Callie saying, "OMG, you guys are adorable together!" I looked away from Ryder and saw that Sharon and Todd were nodding in approval and I felt warm. Not just from what Ryder had said, but because I felt welcomed and loved and I hadn't felt loved in a really long time … if ever.

Then last night's events came to me, when I thought I heard Ryder say, *I love you, sweetheart.* I'd wanted to ask him about it but then I thought better of it because I knew that if he denied it, then I would feel like a complete idiot.

We had comfortable conversations for the rest of dinner and then relaxed in the living room. Well, at least Sharon and I did. Todd, Ryder, and Callie had to clear away and wash all of the dishes, so really I got off easy.

For the rest of the night we watched Thanksgiving movies and cuddled up on the couches and ate dessert, which consisted of a tray of cookies, pumpkin pie, apple pie, and peach cobbler. I didn't understand why we'd made all of those desserts because it was just the five of us. Then I saw the way Ryder and Todd were eating and I looked at Sharon with a look that said *I don't think we made enough.*

Getting ready for bed that night was different because Ryder was planning on staying in his room with me. We each changed into our pajamas, although I was hoping we wouldn't be in them for much longer, and then we were in the bathroom. I put my hair in a bun and scrubbed my face clean of mascara. After drying my face, I looked in the mirror and saw that Ryder was staring at me with a look of want and desire.

Without breaking eye contact, I picked up my toothbrush and applied toothpaste. I turned the faucet on to wet the brush and then sucked the toothbrush into my mouth and moaned. Ryder walked up behind me and placed a hand on my hip.

He put the other one in the waist of my boy shorts inching his way down to where he would find that I was wet and very ready for him.

He placed a thumb on my clit and started to apply a little pressure. I started swaying my hips, trying to get him to push harder but it was as if he was trying to kill me. He leaned down and bit my earlobe. He then whispered in my ear, "Keep brushing your teeth, sweetheart."

I put my hand to the brush and started brushing my teeth. I felt him apply a little more pressure and my knees started to buckle. The hand that was holding my hip moved across my middle and Ryder held me up while he rubbed circles against me.

I tried to ignore the sensations that were going through me and brush my teeth, but I couldn't. His fingers were like magic and I felt like he knew my body better than I did. He knew when to go faster or slow it down to drag out my orgasm and make it last. I wanted to touch him too, but the second I took the toothbrush out of my mouth, Ryder let go of me and went over to his side of the sink and started to brush his teeth.

I was so annoyed and sexually frustrated, but I figured if he wasn't going to finish me off then I would have to do that later. I could feel Ryder staring at me but I ignored him and finished brushing my teeth. I had just spit out my mouthful of toothpaste and started to wipe my mouth when Ryder was behind me and spinning me around.

My mouth met his and he lifted me up onto the bathroom sink. He yanked my tank top off over my head. Before he could move down any further, I put a hand in his boxers and grabbed ahold of him. I heard his moans and grunts in my ear while I moved my hand up and down his velvet cock. Before I knew it, he was lifting me off the sink and carrying me into the bedroom. I thought he was going to place me on the bed, but he sat down on the bed with me still in his lap and scooted back.

My fingers were raking through his hair and I was kissing his neck but Ryder was full of surprises because he pulled me away and said, "Get on your knees, sweetheart." I straddled him and within seconds he was pulling my boy shorts down and I was lifting one leg at a time to get them off easier and quicker. He then told me to get up and he put his hands to his waist and pushed off his boxers.

The second I looked down and saw he was hard and ready, I pushed him on the bed. I moved to put him in my mouth, but Ryder had other things in mind. He pulled me up and twirled me around so he was lying on his back and I was straddling his face. I felt his fingers pushing my lips apart and I heard him suck in a breath because he could see and feel how wet I was.

The second his tongue touched me I bent over and took him into my mouth. I thought it was great last night, but this angle was a lot better. I had a feeling when Ryder and I did have sex that I would love being on top. In this position though, it was like we moved in sync. When I moved my head down he sucked in my clit and when I moved my head up Ryder licked from the opening to my clit. I knew I was getting close and I could tell Ryder was getting close because he started moving up and down and I was deep throating him.

Apparently, I don't have a gag reflex ... Bonus!

I was still bobbing my head up and down when Ryder moaned and grunted and said, "Are you ready, sweetheart?" I was so busy enjoying the taste of his pre-cum and getting as much of him as I could that I moaned in answer. Ryder then went back to sucking my clit and before I knew it, he pushed two fingers inside of me and I saw stars.

I saw rainbows.

Hell, I was experiencing Nirvana.

Then it all came crashing down and Ryder came in my mouth. I sucked him dry and his tongue slathered everything I had to offer. Before I knew it, I was falling on my back and Ryder was crawling up between my legs, kissing me along the way. When his eyes met mine, he gave me a small smile. "Hi."

I giggled and said, "Hi back." I felt like I couldn't move because I was in a euphoric state of bliss. Without any help on my part, Ryder lifted me up into his arms and sat me down so my back was against the headboard. He bent down and I couldn't help but whistle because his ass was a-fucking-mazing.

He turned around with my tank top and shorts in his hand and posed for me. "You like what you see, sweetheart?" I still couldn't form words, so I just said, "Mm hmm." I heard him giggle. "All right, sweetheart, lift your arms." After placing my tank top on me and feeling me up because he just couldn't resist, he then helped me into my shorts and placed a kiss on my lips.

Not the ones on my mouth.

Against my objections, he put his boxers back on, but after seeing how low the boxers were, I was okay with it … I guess. He then scooted in next to me and we spooned and fell into a beautiful sleep.

***

The next morning we had breakfast with everyone. I don't know how Sharon managed, but she made everything and anything you could think of. Pancakes with real maple syrup, waffles with strawberries and whipped cream, bacon, sausage, eggs, buttered toast with your choice of homemade strawberry or grape jam, and finally a fruit salad made up of honeydew, watermelon, strawberries, grapes, and cantaloupe. There was also freshly brewed coffee with cream and sugar, hot tea, and orange juice.

I couldn't believe how amazing it all looked. I grabbed a bowl and a fork because I just wanted some fruit salad and a mug filled with hot coffee. I sat down at the dining room table, and just as I was about to take a bite of honeydew and watermelon, a plate was set in front of me with a waffle topped with strawberries and whipped cream. I looked up and saw Ryder sitting down next to me with a plate filled to the rim with eggs, sausages, and bacon and another plate with pancakes. He took a bite of his eggs and then looked over at me. "Isabelle, you need to eat."

In all honesty, I wasn't that hungry. I leaned over and whispered, "I'd rather eat the strawberries and whipped cream off you." I saw him start to choke on his eggs. He grabbed my hand and put it on his crotch. I took in a shaky breath because he was as hard as a rock, and after he swallowed the food in his mouth, he whispered for my ears only, "We can definitely make that happen and you bet your sweet tasting little pussy we will."

I could feel my cheeks getting red and then I looked over at him and saw that his pupils were dilating. I thought I was going to come right there but I shook the thoughts off and looked away. I took a bite of my food, ignoring Ryder. By this time Todd, Sharon, and Callie were seated at the table, eating their breakfast as well.

Todd was busy reading the morning paper and sipping his coffee. Sharon and Callie were stuck in their own world, talking about going shopping and then going out to lunch to notice what I was about to do.

I don't know what came over me, but I went for it. As soon as Ryder took a bite of his eggs I pushed my hand into his sweatpants and grabbed his erection. He started choking but I kept my hand where it was and just started to move my hand up and down faster. I picked up my coffee cup and pretended to take a sip when in actuality I was giggling into it. I was also wondering how long I could keep this going. That's when I noticed the waffle with whipped cream and strawberries staring at me. I put my coffee cup down and replaced it with a fork and picked up a strawberry and dipped it into the whipped cream.

Ryder must have noticed what I was doing because he said, "Oh God." I turned to Ryder and placed the whipped cream covered strawberry to my lips. I stuck my tongue out, licked that strawberry clean, and then pushed the fork as far as I could into my mouth. I sucked the strawberry off with a loud POP. All the while I was stroking him as hard and as fast as I could manage.

I never took my eyes off Ryder and the second the fork left my mouth he came in my hand.

Oh yeah, breakfast of champions right here!

Chapter 10

After our delicious breakfast, Ryder and I packed up our car and said our goodbyes. It touched me when Sharon grabbed me and pulled me into a hug and whispered in my ear, "Take care of my little boy."

I didn't get to say anything to her because then Callie pulled me into a hug and said, "I can't wait for you guys to come back. You and I will definitely have to hang out then. Hopefully, Sadie and her family will be here next time because I know for a fact she'll love you as much as we do."

Her comment should have made me feel safe and secure but I got really nervous. It was easy, so easy, to fall in love with the Mitchell family. Nevertheless, a part of me wondered if they would still treat me like family if things didn't work out with Ryder and me.

After saying our final goodbyes, Ryder and I got into the truck and started our drive back to school. I looked in the rearview mirror and saw Todd,

Sharon, and Callie waving and a few tears escaping Sharon's eyes. It hurt because I knew they were tears of sadness for her little boy leaving and I had never experienced anything like that. Cynthia hardly even talked to me. When she did, it was just to put me down and make me question every little thing that came into my mind.

We sat in a comfortable silence and just when we pulled onto the highway, the silence was broken. "What are you thinking about, sweetheart?"

I just shrugged my shoulders and said, "Everything."

Ryder looked over at me and quirked his eyebrows. "And by everything, do you mean Cynthia?"

I didn't want to have a deep conversation so I quickly averted the question. "So what's this surprise you have for me, Ryd?"

I heard him chuckle. "All right, sweetheart, I'll let you skip that question but I can't tell you the answer because it's a surprise." I turned to him and gave him my best pleading look but he laughed even harder. "Trust me, sweetheart, just be patient."

The rest of the car ride was comfortable. We sang to the radio and talked about everything. Ryder told me his family really liked me and that they couldn't wait for me to come back and spend time with them. I told him that I'd really enjoyed their company as well.

We were still talking when I noticed that we were getting close to the exit for school but Ryder was in the left lane still going straight. I thought maybe he would get in the right lane to veer off, but he didn't. I turned to him and asked, "Ryder, don't we need to get off here?"

Ryder turned to me with this huge smile on his face and said, "We're on our way to your surprise. I hope you don't mind." I started bouncing up and down and doing a little fist pump and Ryder just laughed at me.

I stopped laughing and looked over at him. "Hey, don't judge me, I'm just excited, is all."

Ryder looked at me. "Who, me? Sweetheart, I'm not judging you whatsoever. You just look so damn cute when you get all excited. That's all."

We only drove maybe an extra ten minutes before he pulled up in front of the tattoo shop where he worked. I looked out the window and then turned back to him. "Why are we here?" Ryder put a hand to my cheek and said, "I finally finished designing your tattoo."

For as long as I could remember, I had always wanted a tattoo but I never knew what to get. There wasn't really anyone who was important enough to me for me to pay tribute them by getting their name on me and I didn't want to get something meaningless. I'd thought about getting one of my favorite quotes but I had way too many favorites to just pick one.

I was broken from my thoughts by Ryder leaning over the console and kissing me on the lips. He pulled back just a little to look in my eyes. "Is this okay? We can do it another time if you want."

I moved my head away and just looked at him. He was so cute when he questioned everything. I wondered if he questioned everything before I came into the picture. I could tell he was nervous because his eyebrows were scrunched together and he was biting on his lower lip. I unbuckled myself, jumped into his lap, and kissed him hard. I kissed down his neck and then pulled back. "This is perfect. Come on, munchkin, let's go."

The shop was closed because of the holiday but Ryder pulled a key out of his pocket and we walked in. He told me that his boss gave him a key to the place because Ryder had explained that he wanted to give me a tattoo and he wanted it to be intimate and private. I blushed. What else were we going to do in here?

Ryder held the door open for me and I walked in. I looked around the shop and took in my new surroundings. The tattoo shop was awesome. There were portfolios of each artist in the place and any design you could think of. There were five stations in the tattoo shop and I also noticed that they did piercings as well. While Ryder was washing his hands and getting the station ready for my tattoo, I looked at all of the pictures in his portfolio.

The tattoos he'd done were incredible. They actually looked real. There were dedications to family members, favorite quotes. The one that really caught my eye was a twenty-three year old guy who got *Team Edward* on his bicep. I started to laugh and Ryder came up behind me and started laughing.

"Yeah, so that guy was dared $5,000 bucks to get the tattoo, and well, as you can see, he did. But don't worry, sweetheart, because yours won't be anything ridiculous like that."

I kept looking at his portfolio and then saw that he also did piercings. Holy shit, I didn't even know you could get pierced in some of those places. I saw normal piercings like ear, nose, and lip, and then I saw some more eccentric ones. Nipples, clit, and a piercing that went right through the dick called a Prince Albert. I didn't even have a dick and I clenched my legs together. And don't even get me started on why in the hell some guy would get his balls pierced.

And then I wondered why you would let someone take a picture of you like that. I mean, if you're going to get your clit pierced, you should at least be freshly shaven or waxed down there. If you're going to have someone take a picture of your pierced dick, then you should at least have something going on down there. That just flabbergasted me.

Ryder must have seen the look on my face because he said, "Don't worry, sweetheart. It only hurts for a little while but then you get over it."

I turned around and looked at him with an eyebrow raised and a hand on my hip. "Oh yeah, how would you know?" He started laughing and then kissed me on the nose. "Because I have one, sweetheart." My mouth dropped but then I thought back to when I went down on him and didn't see anything of the sort pierced.

Ryder just chuckled and said, "I took it out for a while because I didn't want to scare you." I looked up at him and saw this mischievous smile on his face. "Oh, so you automatically assumed I would give you a blow job?"

He just shrugged his shoulders and said, "A guy can wish, can't he?" He took his portfolio out of my hand and threw it on the end table and dragged me over to his station.

I started to get nervous because I saw all different colors of ink and the tattoo gun and then my eyes went directly to the needle. Ryder walked up behind me and kissed the top of my head. "It won't hurt too much, but sweetheart, you have to decide where you want the tattoo. There's a mirror over there."

I walked over to the mirror and looked at my reflection and then back at Ryder. "Can I see the drawing?" Ryder gave me a questioning look before saying, "Uh, no. It's called a surprise, sweetheart." He then stood up from his stool and walked up behind me. He placed his hands at the hem of my shirt and started to drag it up and over my head without taking his eyes off me in the mirror. After my shirt was over my head, he dropped it on the floor and skimmed his fingers down my right side from the top of my rib cage to my hip. "But if you want my opinion, I suggest right there."

I couldn't form words, so I just nodded my head. Cheese and rice. I mean honestly, what couldn't this guy make sexy as hell?

Ryder spun me around and kissed me hard on the mouth, then picked me up and carried me over to his station. He laid me down on the table and I faced him with my right side up. I couldn't take my eyes off him. He washed his hands again and then put latex gloves on. After placing the stencil of the tattoo on my side, Ryder picked out a few colors and then got his gun ready. When he was satisfied, he turned around and scooted over to me on his chair and smiled down at me. "All right, sweetheart, are you ready?"

I smiled up at him. "I trust you." He smiled wide and his eyes were twinkling. He put the gun down by his cart and leaned down to kiss me. The kiss wasn't hard or desire filled. The kiss was soft and intimate and different. He pulled back, kissed me on the tip of my nose, and then winked at me.

I must have made a disappointed noise because he said, "I had to break the kiss or else I would never get your tattoo done today, sweetheart. And trust me when I say, the tattoo is going to take a while." I just laid my head on the table and waited for him to begin. Ryder then picked up his gun and said, "At any point if it gets to be too much to handle tell me to stop and I will. Now deep breaths, sweetheart. In and out." I followed his instructions and then he placed the needle to my skin.

I thought it was going to hurt really bad, but it was like an annoying kind of hurt, plus I was too mesmerized with watching Ryder.

Ryder first did the outline of the tattoo, which hurt like a motherfucker. I had to take a few breaks when he got to the section on my ribs, because I couldn't take it. I told Ryder it really hurt and with a sly grin he said, "I'll kiss it and make it all better." I thought he was going to kiss my freshly inked skin but he leaned up from his chair and gave me a lingering kiss. I started to feel a little tingly and accidently let out a moan.

Ryder chuckled against my mouth. "Not now, sweetheart," and sat back down in his chair. As soon as the worst was over, Ryder began to add the color. Compared to the outline, that took no time at all.

I sat in that chair for eight long hours and not a single minute was I bored because I watched Ryder. I watched how his eyebrows quirked together when he was trying to get something just right. I watched how he bit his lip or when he was in a deep concentration his tongue stuck out between his lips. I loved the way he tilted his head to get different views or when he was humming to himself and didn't realize I was listening.

Before I knew it, he was turning the gun off and applying ointment to my tattoo. After a healthy rub down of my side, Ryder looked into my eyes. "You ready to see your surprise, sweetheart?"

I nodded my head and smiled up at him. "Yeah, I am." Ryder helped me out of the chair, put one hand on my waist, and with the other hand covered my eyes. He walked me over to the mirror. He whispered in my ear, "Close your eyes, sweetheart."

I obediently closed my eyes and he whispered, "Are they closed?"

I just nodded my head because I was filled with so much excitement. Ryder took the hand that was covering my eyes away and then whispered, "All right, sweetheart, you can open your eyes now." I took a deep breath and then I opened my eyes.

I knew that whatever tattoo Ryder gave me would be extraordinary and beautiful but this took my breath away. I couldn't believe how much detail he'd put into it or how it looked so real. I couldn't believe that this piece of art was going to be on me for the rest of my life.

I didn't know where to start because the tattoo was so beautiful. There were flowers with different colors of yellow, pink, peach, and violet staring back at me. They were woven in with leaves going up from my hipbone to the bottom of my breast. I couldn't believe how beautiful they were. I was about to tell Ryder, "Thank you," but then I noticed words woven into the flowers. I couldn't figure out what it said because it was in a different language. I put my hand to the words, *To pepromenon phugein adunaton,* going up my side and traced them.

I looked into Ryder's eyes in the mirror and saw that he was watching my every move. "What does it mean?"

He took a deep breath, and without taking his eyes off me, he said, "It's Greek, and it means '*It's impossible to escape from what is destined.*' I should probably start from the beginning. The flowers on your side are called Ambrosia. The flower is of Greek origin and it's a term which means a returned love. You would think because of its beauty that the Ambrosia is used a lot for romantic gestures, but the Ambrosia is an extremely unappreciated flower and should be cherished by those who have it."

By the end of his explanation I was crying because I couldn't believe that he thought that about me. To Ryder I was his Ambrosia. He saw that I was crying and he spun me around and the look in his eyes was one of distress. He walked over to his station and started cleaning up his supplies. Not looking in my direction again, he said, "Sweetheart, I'm sorry. If you don't like it I can try and fix it or hide it or something. It's just that you told me to design something for you and I wanted to surprise you."

He slammed his hand against the wall. "FUCK!" I jumped at his reaction. I walked over to him and wrapped my arms around his middle while he was still turned away from me.

Ryder let out a breath and then I saw his head fall. I almost couldn't hear him because he was whispering, but he said, "I'm sorry."

I didn't understand what was going on. I walked around to stand in front of him. "Ryder, do you think I don't like the tattoo?"

He looked at me like I was dumb or something. "You were crying, Isabelle. What was I supposed to think?"

I giggled and put a hand to the back of his neck and pulled his head down to mine. He closed his eyes. It was like he didn't want to see the look in my eyes when I told him that I hated it.

I kissed him on his nose. "Ryder, please open your eyes." He hesitated but then did as I asked. I looked into his eyes and then smiled.

"Ryder, I cried not because I hated the tattoo but because I loved it. I feel like the word love doesn't even come close to how I feel about the tattoo you just gave me. In fact, there are no words to describe how I feel about this tattoo. Your explanation and your thought concept was just beautiful. I wasn't expecting anything like this at all." He flinched when I said that but I kept going. "I thought a simple quote or image would have sufficed but you exceeded my expectations. In fact, you crushed them." I wrapped both hands around his neck to pull him closer for a kiss. After my lips left his, I looked straight in his eyes. "You, Ryder Mitchell, have a true gift right here and I am incredibly proud that I was able to receive a tattoo which you designed specifically for me. I feel incredibly lucky to have it and to know that I'm the only one who will have it is … well, I don't have words for it. I just want you to know that I will cherish it for the rest of my life."

The second the words left my lips Ryder pulled me to him and kissed me. I opened my greedy little mouth and sucked his lower lip in. I heard him groan and then he lifted me up into his arms and walked me over to his table. He sat me on the table and stood in between my legs. He kissed me one more time and then put his hands on either side of my face. "You are incredible, Isabelle. As much as I want you right here, right now, I have to put some wrap on your tattoo. Okay?"

As much as I wanted him right this moment as well, I let out a frustrated breath and nodded. It would have been totally fine with me if he'd bent me over that tattoo chair and had his way with me because then he would remember it every time he worked. All that really mattered to me was that I cared about the person and at this moment I wanted it to be with Ryder.

After Ryder bandaged me up, we left the shop and picked up some dinner from a local fast food place and went on home. We were tired from our eventful day so we just left our luggage in the car and relaxed on the couch for the rest of the night, cuddled in one another's arms.

Chapter 11

The rest of Thanksgiving break seemed to fly right by like the snap of my fingers. Although it was only a week, it was the best week of my life. Not only did Ryder take care of me every day by applying cream and lotion to my tattoo but he took care of me in other ways as well. The best part of our week was making an inside tent in the living room using the dining room table chairs and the bar stools and eating tons of junk food. We used a bunch of blankets and pillows and it looked like a cabana.

You can't have a tent without s'mores and we decided to go MacGyver and make them on the kitchen stove. I think making the s'mores was the best part. At some point after taking a bite of the mixture of crumbly graham cracker, gooey chocolate, and burnt marshmallow, I got some on the side of my lip. Not only did Ryder swipe it off with his tongue but he made me scream his name over and over again on the kitchen counter.

We also watched all the movies that we could think of like *Horrible Bosses*, *The Perks of Being a Wallflower* and *Pitch Perfect*. We listened to music like Mumford and Sons and The Lumineers. I also showed him a couple of books of mine that I thought he should read. He said he would read anything but, "I will not read about whips and chains and billionaires. I'm not a middle-aged housewife." I just laughed and told him that I wasn't a middle-aged housewife and had practically creamed my panties reading those books.

***

The first day back from Thanksgiving break had to be a Monday. I managed to go to my first class with Ryder and then Sarah, Jade, Ashlynn, and I had our lunch date at the café. After we all got our lunches and sat down, we all discussed our Thanksgiving breaks.

I told them about meeting Ryder's family and the tattoo he gave me. Jade informed us that she and Jason had an *okay* break and left it at that, which made Sarah, Ashlynn, and myself a bit curious. I could tell that we all wanted to ask her what happened because we could tell from her demeanor that it was bad but we didn't want to intrude. Ashlynn told us how she had a quiet break with her family. She hung out with her friends from school and got caught up on some books that she'd been dying to read. She told me that she definitely recommended *The Sea of Tranquility* and that the ending was the best part. She also mentioned a book called *Easy* and promised that I would love both Lucas and Landon.

Then it was Sarah's turn. We all waited for her to tell us *all* about her break. That's when she shoved her left hand in our direction and screamed, "I'M GOING TO BE MRS. GABE PRESCOTT!" We all started screaming—it was an afterthought that we were in the café. We were probably getting stares and comments. But who gave a shit? Our best friend was engaged!

We inundated her with questions. When did he ask? How did he ask? Did he ask for permission?

Sarah just laughed and said, "All right, bitches, sit down and let me talk and I'll tell you." We followed her instructions and she explained that Gabe did ask for permission. Since her dad had passed away, Gabe asked for her mom and her little brother's permission. He thought it was important to ask the both of them because he didn't just want her mom's blessing, but also Sarah's little brother's as well. After all, if everyone said yes, then he'd be in their family for a long time.

The ring Gabe picked out was absolutely gorgeous; it was a two-carat white princess cut diamond with three little pink diamonds on either side.

"It was so romantic," Sarah said. Her eyes grew distant as she recounted the details for us. It was almost like we were there with her. "He took me to the baseball field at the high school. We sat up in the bleachers, just talking and joking while we enjoyed our favorite ice cream…mint chocolate chip. "Suddenly, Gabe turned to me and asked, 'Do you remember the first words I said to you?'"

Sarah started chuckling. "I replied, 'Yeah, I do. It went something like, 'I'm jealous Ryder has a beautiful girl cheering him on. Do you want to change that for me, beautiful?'

"Gabe started chuckling at my impression because it really sucked. Then he got really serious. 'Do you want to cheer each other on for the rest of our lives?' I was so taken aback I didn't realize what he meant at first. 'Gabe, what are you talking about?'" Sarah laughed. We were all wrapped up in the moment, mouths open, eyes wide.

"Gabe turned to me and said, 'Sarah Thompson, I have wanted to marry you for as long as I can remember. I will forever cheer you on whether you want to become a clown or a politician. I just ask you to promise me something. Promise me that you will make me the happiest man ever by marrying me. Sarah Thompson, will you marry me?'

"I couldn't believe I hadn't caught on! I didn't say the traditional response, 'Yes, I'll marry you.' What fun is there in that? Instead, I jumped up and straddled him right there on the bleachers and said, 'Hell, yeah, I'll marry you, Gabe Prescott!'"

My eyes welled up with tears. Still, I couldn't help but laugh because Sarah's answer was definitely a very Sarah way of doing things.

We each congratulated her. Ashlynn said, "Congratulations, Sarah."

"You and Gabe are going to make fine ass babies," Jade added.

"You're going to have a beautiful wedding and a beautiful life together," I said. Sarah then informed us that we were each going to be in her wedding. The excitement began all over again.

Once lunch was over, Sarah and I headed to our next class together. "Can I ask you something, Isabelle?" she asked.

"Sarah, you can ask me anything. What's up?"

It looked like Sarah was really nervous. She was playing with a strand of her hair and biting on her lower lip. I stopped her in her tracks, stepped in front of her, and started shaking her shoulders. "Sarah, what's going on? Talk to me!"

Sarah looked at me. "All right, I'm just going to come out with it. Iz, will you be my Maid of Honor? I know we haven't known each other for a long time, but I feel like you and I really get each other. I promise I won't be one of those Bridezillas and if I do go down *that* path, I know you'll be there to whip my ass and slap me across the face to bring me back to reality. Please?"

She started to pucker her bottom lip and she looked so pathetic I laughed at her. "Yes, Sarah. Stop begging because I will be your Maid of Honor, but—" I held up my pointer finger in front of her, "—on one condition! I won't allow you to choose ugly bridesmaids' dresses and certainly not an ugly Maid of Honor dress. Now if you can agree with me on that, then I'll be your Maid of Honor."

Sarah immediately wrapped her arms around my neck and pulled me into a hug. "Yes, Isabelle! Yes!" We immediately started jumping up and down in each other's arms, not giving a flying fuck who was staring at us. We were way too excited because of Sarah's engagement and me becoming her Maid of Honor to care!

After my last class was over for the day I headed home. Home. I hadn't been able to call a place that in a long time. Maybe ever. I pulled into the apartment complex, put my car in park, and just sat there in the driver's seat for a few minutes, thinking back on the last couple of months.

I couldn't believe how fast my life had changed. I had left Cynthia's house in August, wanting my life to change. Still, I had never planned on it changing this drastically. And by *drastically,* I meant a good thing. In fact, a very good thing. I couldn't help but smile at how different everything had become.

I got out of my car, grabbed my bag, and headed upstairs to our apartment. I found my house key and put it in the lock and turned.

Click.

I opened the door and froze because what I found completely blew my mind and left me speechless.

Ryder was standing in the kitchen cooking dinner. He had on an apron and, good Lord, it was the sexiest vision I think I had ever seen. I walked into the apartment, closing the door behind me as quietly as I could without taking my eyes off Ryder. Thankfully, Ryder's back was to me so I just leaned against the front door with my arms crossed and watched him.

He had his iPod plugged into speakers while he was cooking. He was singing along to the songs. The current song playing was *I'd Rather Be With*

You by Joshua Radin. I had always loved that song and the simplicity of it, but hearing Ryder sing it was a completely different experience. He was putting so much soul into it.

You know how some singers sing the words but they don't necessarily listen to the words that are coming out of their mouths? Ryder didn't sing that way; he took it to a whole new level. It felt like he wasn't just singing to *any girl* but to me. I felt and heard it in the way he was singing and then with the last lyrics he sang my name. I was speechless but I didn't want Ryder catching me, so I waited for him to get twenty seconds into *Teach Me How to Dougie* and opened the front door really quietly and closed it just loud enough for Ryder to hear me. I couldn't hold in my laughter because he spun around really fast and almost knocked over whatever he was cooking on the stove. His face turned really red. "You're home early, Isabelle."

I walked over to the breakfast bar and sat down on a stool. "Yeah, I was supposed to work but Mrs. Bee said that I could just go home because Ashlynn had it covered, so here I am. Why? Do you have a date or something?" I was being a little smartass and joking around with him. Ryder put the spatula back in the pan and said, "Yeah, with this really beautiful girl. You know her? She has this chocolate brown silky hair and these amazing hazel eyes that twinkle. She's incredibly funny, extremely smart, and has a fascination with reading and drinking white wine." Ryder walked over to me and started to cage me in to my seat with his arms. He bit my earlobe and whispered in my ear, "And I bet you I can make her come in less than the seven minutes it'll take for our dinner to be ready."

Almost instantly I got goose bumps, my nipples hardened, and my panties were soaked. I turned around in his arms and kept my hands in between my legs. As I looked up into his eyes I quirked an eyebrow. I wanted to play this scene out as long as I could manage. "You bet, huh? What exactly do you bet, munchkin?"

Without blinking, Ryder said, "My heart," and then he picked me up, took me back to his room and had me screaming his name in less than five minutes.

After making our way from the bedroom to the dining room, Ryder had me sit down and he portioned everything out on two plates. He handed me one before setting his down and getting us each a drink. He got me a glass of white wine and a beer for himself. Once he sat down and settled in we both started to eat.

For dinner Ryder had made a sauté of vegetables that consisted of broccoli, asparagus, corn, and chopped carrots. There was also brown rice and this amazingly juicy chicken with a brown sauce. With each bite it seemed like it got better and better and I couldn't help but moan my way through dinner. Halfway through our meal, Ryder picked me up from my chair and carried me back into the bedroom saying, "The only moaning you'll be making is when I'm licking you and my fingers are inside you, sweetheart," and that's exactly what he did.

After we finally finished dinner, Ryder asked if I had any room for dessert and I nodded. Before he could get up I was bent in front of him, unbuckling and unzipping his jeans and taking him in my mouth. I put one hand at his base and before long I tasted his pre-cum in my mouth. I played with his balls and gently squished and pulled them in one hand and with the other I had him in a firm grasp and stroked him up and down.

I could hear Ryder moaning, "Ah, fuck." While I loved hearing him moan, I wanted to hear him yell when he came, so I sucked him into my mouth and stroked him hard and fast. While he laid back I looked up into his dark, bold eyes. He seemed to like me being in control. For the most part I liked Ryder to be in control. But this? This turned me on. I liked being the dominant one right now.

The way he begged and pleaded for me to go faster. The smell of his arousal and the salty taste. The way his stomach tightened and his cock got harder. My mouth watered. I couldn't believe how sexy he was. To know that I was the one doing this to him was empowering.

With his hands lightly playing with my hair I fucked his cock with my mouth. Within seconds he was yelling, "FUCK, ISABELLE!"

The last time he was getting ready to come in my mouth he had warned me and tried to get me to move away. This time he couldn't warn me but I was completely fine with it. I loved the taste of him and how he came in my mouth. The salty liquid squirting into the back of my throat. The smells were musky and manly. He started moving his hips in my direction. I sucked him far into my mouth and sucked as hard as I could. Then he yelled, "ISABELLE!" and pushed his cock all the way in my throat. Feeling his cum squirt in my mouth gave me relief. Slowly I moved my mouth up and down his shrinking cock. I loved watching his body twitch and hearing his gasping for air. When I was satisfied that I had gotten every last drop, I released his cock from my mouth and swallowed it down. Closing my eyes, I released a little moan as I swallowed the creamy liquid.

I had always heard stories about how girls hated giving their boyfriend or fuck-buddy head. I think maybe they just didn't know how to give a proper blow job. Because if you got your man to twitch and gasp for air, to beg and plead for you to make him come, you would love it! I loved having his taste in my mouth and how I could make him yell my name. Licking the base of his cock up to the tip one last time, I then looked up into his eyes. They were smoldering. His nostrils were flared from his deep breathing and his mouth was slight opened.

A part of me wanted to kiss him but I didn't know if he would want to taste himself on me. As I was getting ready to wipe my hand across my face he grabbed me by my upper arms, dragged me onto his lap, and manhandled me with his lips. His tongue was in my mouth before I could even think straight and he was ravenous. This was no simple kiss, it was like he was fucking me with his mouth.

He slowly moved one hand to wrap around my waist and then put one up my shirt and under my bra. He started pinching and pulling a nipple between his coarse fingers. I was completely caught up in the kiss. He rolled the nipple a little harder then moved to do the same to the other nipple. When Ryder touched my soft nipple I gasped for air. My stomach started to tighten and my eyes fluttered closed. I couldn't believe how amazing it felt having him touch my nipples that way. I licked my lips as I imagined him sucking on my nipples. My head fell back and I could feel myself tightening. I needed a release so I started to grind against him.

"Are you going to come, baby?" Ryder asked while the other hand traveled up my shirt and under my bra.

"Uh huh," I moaned. With my hands on his shoulders and legs on either side of him, I grinded into him. I knew I was close. I could feel it. The tightening of my lower stomach. My heart beating rapidly. My panties moistening. The second I felt my legs quiver I knew this was going to be a powerful orgasm.

"Come for me, baby," Ryder said before sucking on my neck. Grasping my nipples in his coarse fingers, he squeezed.

Moving his mouth up to mine, Ryder kissed my lips one last time. I couldn't think. I couldn't breathe right. I started to shake in his arms.

Keeping a firm grip on me Ryder whispered, "Calm down sweetie," before kissing the side of my mouth.

As I attempted to catch my breath I wondered what it would be like when we actually did have sex.

Ryder gave me slow kisses along my neck and shoulders before he pulled back to look at me. "You know, I was seriously meaning we had dessert, but damn, that was incredible. I mean, Isabelle, you have me speechless right now."

I just giggled and said, "Well, I'm glad you liked it." He glanced at me then a look of bewilderment came across his face. "Isabelle, I didn't like it."

I felt like he slapped me across the face with his words and I flinched. I wanted to get off his lap as fast as I could but he tightened his hold on me and said, "Isabelle, *like* doesn't even come close to how I felt in that moment. Hell, how I feel in *this* moment. Fuck, how I feel in every moment that I spend with you."

I felt relieved and kissed him on the lips. "Come on, munchkin. I'm ready for some actual dessert now." I got off his lap and headed into the kitchen. I heard him buttoning and zipping up his jeans behind me and giggled. I couldn't believe the way Ryder was making me change so fast, and I liked it.

I opened the fridge to see strawberry shortcake and a wide smile spread across my face. I remembered the morning at his parents' house with the whipped cream and strawberries comment. Ryder must have known what I was thinking because he kissed me on my neck and said, "Soon. Very soon. But for the rest of the night I want to talk and cuddle with you, sweetheart." He reached out in front of me and grabbed the glasses. He made his way into the living room, and after he sat down, he turned on the television for some background noise. I pulled out two spoons and just looked at the view and smiled.

Blinking a few times, I made my way to the couch and cuddled up with Ryder. After taking a few bites, another thought from the short time we spent at his parents' surfaced in my mind. "Hey, Ryder, I have a question for you."

He took a huge bite of his strawberry shortcake. "Shoot."

"You said that the flower *Ambrosia* I have tattooed on my side means *love requited*, right?"

Ryder stopped eating and put his glass down and turned to look at me. "Yeah?"

I put my glass down because I wanted to give him my undivided attention. "We had a discussion earlier this semester on what we each thought about love."

He gave a small smile. "Yeah, I remember. Why do you bring it up?"

I looked down in my lap and started playing with my fingers. "I never asked you who exactly you were talking about because I didn't think it was any of my business …"

Ryder placed a hand under my chin and lifted it so I was looking at him. "But?"

"But I need to know now. Who was it you were talking about?"

He smiled. "I think you know who I was talking about, *Isabelle*."

The way he said my name made me think that I was right but I still had to have an answer. "I have a theory but I'd rather you give me an answer. I won't be disappointed if I'm wrong but I have to know." I started biting the corner of my lower lip because I was so nervous.

Ryder placed a hand on either side of my face and right before he kissed me. "You."

Chapter 12

To me, Christmas was just like any normal day on the calendar. Growing up, I never really got to experience Christmas unless it was watching Christmas movies on television. I loved the simplicity of Christmas and how it used to be. It used to be just about spending time with your loved ones and opening a few gifts. However, over the years it's become something more commercial.

In my twenty years I had never bought a gift for someone because until I came to school, it was just Cynthia, and I would never buy anything for her. I remember when I was little I always heard the other kids in my class talking about how amazing Christmas was. They got brand new bikes, Barbie dolls, and games. I remember always hearing my classmates complaining about how they got clothes, but something that those kids took for granted I would have killed for. Until I was old enough to get a job, my wardrobe consisted of shoes with holes in them, jeans, shirts that were too small, and donated winter coats.

Even if Cynthia could've afforded better, I was a nuisance to her and I didn't matter. Looking back, I realize how sad my childhood was and if I ever do have kids, I won't let them feel that way. I plan to let them know how much I love them each and every day.

For as long as I live, I will never forget this one Christmas. I was maybe five years old.

***

Walking out into the living room on Christmas morning, I feel my heart beating rapidly. I can't wait to see what Mommy and Santa got me for Christmas this year. I really want that new Barbie doll with the pretty pink dress and glitter heels. Or maybe the new tennis shoes with the wheels on the bottom.

I start to tiptoe down the stairs because Mommy wasn't feeling good last night and I don't want to give her a headache. Especially on Christmas. After all, it's the best day of the year. I do hope she's feeling better today, though. As I walk through the kitchen, I hear snoring coming from the living room. I feel bad that Mommy fell asleep on the couch again. She does that a lot when she drinks her juice. I want some of the juice but I can only have apple juice.

Quietly walking into the living room, I see there's nothing here. I wonder if maybe Mommy put them somewhere else? But there's always Santa.

What if he didn't know how to get in here because we don't have a chimmey, or whatever you call it. I head over to Mommy to ask her if she's okay, but I see her begin to wake up.

I'm standing in the middle of the living room holding my hands as I patiently wait for her to yawn and stretch. I begin to open my mouth to say something but Mommy lifts the juice bottle from the floor and takes a big gulp. Then she takes out one of her candy cigarettes and starts playing with it.

I don't understand why she likes them so much because they smell really gross. I smell like it all the time and the kids at school make fun of me. They say I'm dirty and I don't know how to get clean. They all say I have cooties, but what I don't get is even the girls say it. I thought only boys had cooties? Not me.

Once Mommy takes another huge sip of her juice, she looks over at me and yells, "Well? What do you want?"

I jump back. I don't know why she's angry with me. I want to cry but maybe she still isn't feeling good. Taking in a deep breath I ask, "Are you okay, Mommy?" Sometimes she looks at me like she doesn't like me. I don't know what I do so wrong. Maybe it's because I accidentally left her Christmas card and present at school. I made her a card with all types of glitter. I even drew a rainbow on the inside. It was hard, but Mommy is worth it.

Her present was a story I wrote. I wrote about a princess and how her mommy rules the kingdom. I wrote about how pretty the mommy is and how I want the mommy to find a daddy. I don't know my daddy, but at least I have my mommy. She's not perfect, but neither am I. Or at least that's what Mommy says.

Screaming at me again, Mommy asks, "What do you want?" I feel tears coming but I try to blink them away and say, "It's Christmas, Mommy." She takes another sip of her juice and starts laughing. I think maybe Mommy is playing a joke on me and she hid the presents. Kind of like buried treasure and we're the pirates. I start to laugh along with Mommy but she asks, "What are you laughing at?"

Still giggling, I say, "You hid the presents." She starts laughing again and puts the candy cigarette in her mouth and says, "Nope. I just didn't get you anything." I feel wetness on my face and try to wipe them away but Mommy starts laughing again and says, "All you do is cry. You're a bad child and that's why I didn't get you anything. Hell, you didn't even get me anything, you selfish brat."

I hate it when she calls me a brat. I know I'm not supposed to say the word "hate" because it's a bad word but I don't care. I just … I really don't like it.

I mean, I know I don't listen all the time and I know that I only get okay grades in school. I'll admit that sometimes I read my books way too much but I don't think I'm as bad as Mommy says. I bring my hands up to my face and try to wipe away the tears but I hear Mommy laugh again. Taking my hands away from my face, I hear her say, "You're such a damn cry baby." Lifting the juice to her lips, she takes another sip and says, "It's only fair. You didn't get me anything so I didn't get you anything."

After taking a deep breath I say, "I made you a card and I wrote you a story but I accidentally left it at school, Mommy." I head toward her because I want to give her a hug. I think maybe she's just not feeling well. Maybe she has the flu or something, but as I walk over to her and try to wrap my arms around her, she pushes me away. It's enough for me to fall on my butt.

She looks down at me and says, "I don't want a stupid card or a story, brat. You know what I want?"

I shake my head and begin to stand up again. Taking another gulp of her juice, she says, "Of course you don't know what I want. I want you out of here. You were a mistake and I can't believe I'm stuck with you. I should have gotten an abortion when I had the chance. Now, when I get my Christmas gift, you can have yours. Does that sound like a deal?"

I don't know what an abortion is but I can tell Mommy is really mad at me. Sometimes I think she hates me and we all know that hate is a bad word. Quickly getting to my feet, I run out of the living room. Mommy is laughing really hard. Running up the stairs, I curl up under my covers and make a promise to myself that I will never let this happen again.

***

When I got older and got a job, I would have my own little Christmases. I was always extremely careful with my money and how I spent it.

Throughout the year I would just get the basic necessities but my birthday and Christmas were different. I would go out on a little shopping spree, buying a few pairs of jeans, shirts, and shoes. Of course they were all from thrift shops or second hand stores, but to me they were brand new. If I really wanted to splurge, I got a couple of books to keep me busy over Christmas break. And while most families were having turkey, I was ordering Chinese takeout and getting Ben and Jerry's Crème Brulee ice cream.

But now I have people I can buy Christmas presents for. I want to get everybody a little something but I really want to go all out for Ryder. Not only is he my boyfriend, but in my time of need he offered a helping hand, and not just anybody would do that. It wouldn't even matter if they got me anything. All that matters to me is that I had people I could actually give a gift to.

***

Ashlynn and I decided to do our Christmas shopping after we got off work at the library. We went to the mall and looked around for ideas for everybody's Christmas gifts. I had already gotten Sarah, Gabe, and Ashlynn's gifts, and I had to order Ryder's gifts off the internet. Since Ryder wasn't making me pay for rent, I was able to save up my money. I figured since I had finally found a family, I wanted to get them all extravagant gifts. I had never been able to do this before. Yes, I may have splurged just a little bit, but it was all worth it in the end. I couldn't wait to see all of the smiles on their faces. Especially Ryder's.

Currently, we were in Spencer's because I was looking for Jade's gift. I decided to get her a Sex Positions book and a little something extra because I knew she would love it. After picking up the book, I decided to go into the costume department and saw this really cute Santa outfit.

Hmmm, this could be a good idea.

I was looking at the costume when this guy walked up to me. "You know, if you want to try that out, I'd be a willing participant." I turned to yell at the guy but he was actually really good looking. He was around the same height as Ryder. While Ryder was majorly built, this guy was leaner but still had muscles. He had bright blue eyes and curly brown hair with an eyebrow ring. He must have noticed I was staring at him because his lips turned up into this cocky grin.

Immediately, I went back to looking at the costume, and without looking at him, I said, "Sorry, but the position has already been filled."

"Well, damn, that is some lucky bastard. I'm Neil, by the way." I turned to look at him and shook his hand. "Isabelle. Nice to meet you, Neil." I tried to pull my hand back but he kept ahold of it. "You too, Isabelle," he said. He let go of my hand and disappeared before I could say anything.

Ashlynn ran up to me. "Who the hell was that good looking guy?"

I looked at her and shrugged my shoulders. "His name is Neil. He saw what I was holding and started hitting on me." Ashlynn made some grumbling noise. "Why is it that you get the guy of your dreams and still have good looking guys checking you out? Meanwhile I can't even get Jason to notice me!"

I just patted her on the shoulder. "Don't worry, Ashlynn. Jason just has his head so far up his ass he hasn't seen what's right in front of him. But trust me when I say he will notice, and if he doesn't, then he's a jackass!" I saw Ashlynn smile and then she laughed. "You're right! I should just move on and forget about him." Ashlynn decided on some edible lube and furry pink handcuffs for Jade's gift.

***

"Sweetheart, what did you want to do tonight?" We were cuddled on the couch and Ryder was watching a movie on television while I was half watching the movie and reading a book.

I put the book down. "I don't know. What'd you have in mind?"

Ryder turned the television off and faced me. "I was thinking maybe we could go ice skating or snow tubing if you wanted."

"I've never been ice skating before."

"You've never been ice skating before?" I laughed and then nodded. Before I could say anything else, Ryder was on his way back to his bedroom and yelling back to me to get changed because we were leaving to go ice skating in a couple of minutes. He told me to dress warmly because the skating rink was outside. I decided on jeans and a sweatshirt with my winter coat. I also had on some heavy socks with boots, gloves, and a scarf.

After we each changed, we hopped in the car and were on our way to the skating rink. Once we got there and paid for our skates, we were near the entrance to the rink. Ryder stepped on first and then turned to me and put his hands out. "Come on, sweetheart. I won't let you go."

I put my hands in his and before I stepped out onto the rink, I said, "You promise?"

Without blinking, he said, "Yes."

I was way too scared to actually skate, so for a few minutes Ryder skated backwards pulling me along. He laughed at how I held his hands in a death grip. But after a while, I started to get a little braver.

"Okay, I think I'm ready to just hold your hand like a normal person."

Ryder laughed. "Sweetheart, you are anything but normal. But if you're ready, then okay." He let go of my one hand and we started skating along together. We were skating at a snail's pace, but whatever.

For a while we skated in complete silence, watching the other people skating. Parents teaching their kids how to skate. Couples holding hands and skating together. Friends skating with one another. And my least favorite, the people who were skating by themselves, showing off.

Ryder squeezed my hand. "So, sweetheart, you know how my parents invited us to come for Christmas?"

"Yeah. Why, what's up?"

"Well, there might be a change of plans."

"What do you mean? Do they not want me to come?"

Ryder pulled me in close, wrapped his arm around my shoulder and then kissed me on the cheek. "Isabelle, sweetheart, it's nothing like that. I just had an idea and I wanted to run it by you."

"Oh. What's the idea ?"

I turned to look at Ryder, and while his face was red from the cold, I could also tell that he was blushing. Ryder blushing is probably the cutest thing I have ever seen. "Well, um, I thought we could stay at the apartment and have Christmas there. You know, just the two of us?"

Next thing I knew I was falling down. Ryder tried to help me stand, but he fell down and pulled me along with him. For a second we just laid there laughing but then Ryder realized he was lying on the floor of the skating rink. "Jesus Christ, I'm freezing!" I started to get up but Ryder wrapped his arms around my waist to keep me there. "Sweetheart, it was just an idea. If you don't want to, we don't have to. I just thought it would be nice."

"I'm not going to lie. The idea sounds like a good one. I mean, if you still want to?" I'd been nervous about spending Christmas with his family. After I saw that Santa costume, I decided that I wanted to have sex with Ryder on Christmas Eve. It would have been really awkward having sex with him for the first time with his parents sleeping at the end of the hall.

Ryder smiled really big and said, "Hell, yeah, I still want to! But um, sweetheart, can we get up? My ass cheeks are frozen together."

"Oh no, we can't have that now, can we?"

We decided to get some hot chocolate to warm up our frozen bodies. They were offering regular and peppermint, so Ryder got regular and I got peppermint so could share. Ryder had an arm wrapped around me and was moving it up and down against me. "You warm enough, sweetheart?"

I just snuggled into him and murmured against his body, "Yes." I took another sip of my peppermint hot chocolate. "Can I try yours?" I started to hand him my cup but he pulled my face to his and swept his tongue in my mouth and kissed me.

I kind of forgot where we were and moved to sit on his lap to kiss him deeper. He wrapped his arms around my waist and pulled me as close as he could. I moaned and then heard him groan against me. Then some kids started chuckling and one yelled, "Get a room!"

I pulled away, blushing, but it didn't faze Ryder. He looked at the kids and said, "Can you blame me?"

My face was buried in Ryder's chest so I just heard a lot of, "No ways," "Absolutely nots," and even a, "She's smokin' hot!"

Ryder was laughing but he corrected them, "No. She's beautiful." I kissed him again on the lips.

"All right, stud, what do you want to do now?" Ryder squeezed me around the waist and said, "I was thinking we could get our own Christmas tree.

Oh and by the way—" he kissed me again. "I love the peppermint hot chocolate."

***

"So which one do you want, sweetheart?" Ryder and I were walking hand in hand, looking at the Christmas trees. While they were all beautiful, none of them were really the "It" tree. We were getting ready to leave when I saw the best tree there. I let go of Ryder's hand and ran towards the tree. "I want this one." Ryder walked over to me and started laughing. "Isabelle, this tree looks like it's going to die. How about we at least pick a tree that will last us until Christmas?" He started moving me to a different tree but I stood my ground. "No. I want this one. I think it's beautiful and besides, no one wants it. All the trees in this lot are going to die eventually." I poked out my bottom lip and looked up at Ryder from under my eyelashes.

He waved his hand back and forth. "Oh no! Don't even think about the pouty lip, sweetheart, because it won't work." I walked over to him really slow and ran a hand from his abs up to the back of his neck. I pulled his head down to mine so he was eye level with me. In a husky voice, I whispered, "What about this?"

I sucked in his lower lip and then lightly bit down on it and heard him moan. He pulled me right up against him where I could feel how badly he wanted me. I wrapped my arms around his neck. When he stuck his tongue in my mouth, I sucked hard. I leaned back and looked at him and saw that his expression was one of sexual desire. I moved back to kiss his lips but at the last second, I kissed the side of his mouth, then his jaw, and then his neck. I felt the vibrations of his moans against my lips. I then licked his neck and bit that same exact spot. I felt Ryder push me back and I wondered what I did wrong but he said, "All right, after that you can have whatever the fuck you want." He waved me away and said, "Go get the tree, Charlie Brown."

We ended up getting the tree free. After loading it on the top of Ryder's car, we went to get decorations and lights. Back at our apartment, Ryder carried the tree up while I got the bags of decorations. After taking off our jackets, we decided to change into something more comfortable.

Ryder got the tree up and put the lights on while I made some sandwiches for us and got chips and drinks. Ryder walked towards the tree and plugged the cord in, and like magic, all of the lights turned on. I knew Ryder was hungry, so I told him to sit down and eat while I got started on decorating the tree. Even though I was hungry, I wanted to decorate the tree more because it was so foreign to me.

I was in the middle of placing a red ornament on the tree when Ryder said, "I feel like this is going to be the best Christmas yet."

I walked over and sat down on the coffee table facing him. "Why do you say that?"

He set his sandwich down and pulled me onto his lap and kissed me. And as simple as breathing he said, "Because you're here."

Chapter 13

Sarah and Gabe decided to throw a Christmas party at their apartment the night before Winter Break. It was just our core group of friends and we had decided to get everyone in the group a gift. At first we thought about doing Secret Santa but opted against it. To make it more festive and get everybody in the holiday mood we all had to wear ugly Christmas sweaters. Ryder was dressed in a brown sweater with a stocking attached to it that read, *I've been a Bad Boy* and I was wearing a red sweater that read, *All I got for Christmas was this Fucking Sweater!*

Walking next door, we could hear Christmas music blasting. I was about to knock on the door when Ryder just opened it and walked in. I almost wanted to leave the second I walked in because it looked like Santa and Mrs. Claus lived there. From the top of the walls to the carpeting there was something Christmas related. Christmas music was playing and currently muted on television was

Rudolph the Red Nosed Reindeer. There were nutcrackers and elves on the counter of the breakfast bar and stockings hanging along the side.

Even the food was Christmas themed. There were Christmas cookies in the shapes of Santa Claus, Rudolph, and candy canes. They all looked professionally decorated. The frosting was perfect and the cookies actually looked real.

When I try and frost a cookie or a cupcake, the icing gets all over my fingers and I just give up. I figured they wouldn't go to all this trouble and not have a gingerbread house, so I started to look around the apartment and spotted a gorgeous gingerbread house. The gumdrops were neatly placed on the roof with Sweet Tarts. The path leading up to the house was neatly covered in an array of candies. Sarah had even made a candy cane lamppost. I went over to the perfect little gingerbread house and took a gumdrop off the rooftop. I stuck the gumdrop in my mouth to hide the evidence and saw Gabe watching me. He started laughing.

After swallowing the chewy gumdrop, I walked back over to the food display. There was a cheese tray in the shape of a Christmas tree along with Christmas tree crackers, bacon wrapped scallops, quiche, and shrimp with cocktail sauce. There were some pretty awesome drinks like the Grinch martini, candy cane shooters, and, my favorite, Boozy Peppermint Hot Chocolate. Not only was it delicious but so were the memories that came with the beverage. After filling up on some of the yummy hot chocolate, I walked around the room to look at all of the decorations and then stopped at the sight of the tree.

Holy Moses! I thought my tree decorating skills were good but they were shit compared to Sarah and Gabe's tree. Every ornament was put in its rightful place and the tinsel was thrown about the tree like a professional decorator did it. The tree looked like it came from a magazine shoot.

Ryder followed my gaze and said, "Yeah, Sarah is a little crazy about Christmas."

I looked at him and let out a breath. "Ya think?"

Ryder didn't say anything because the next thing I knew he was sweeping me off my feet and planting his lips to mine. I wrapped my arms around him and nibbled on his lower lip and then felt his tongue against my own. We got a little carried away and then I heard someone yell, "Get it!"

I laughed against his mouth and pulled back. "What was that for, munchkin?"

Ryder kissed me again, set me down, and pointed above his head. "Mistletoe, it's tradition—" then he leaned in so only I could hear the rest of what he had to say, "plus I saw you drinking the peppermint hot chocolate and I just couldn't resist."

After hanging out for a while, Sarah said, "All right, guys, let's go in the living room and open up presents." One at a time we went around the room and gave each other our gifts. Earlier, Ryder and I had decided we would give our gifts to one another on Christmas day.

I got a basket filled with a Rabbit vibrator and some lotion and oils from Jade, perfume from Jason, *The Sea of Tranquility* from Ashlynn, a shirt

161

from Gabe that read *I Know How to Handle My Man's Baseballs and Bat* and a shirt from Sarah that read:

Maid of Honor (noun)
Definition – Bride's BITCH
I, Isabelle, am Sarah's Maid of Honor!

Jade turned to Ryder and mouthed, "You're very welcome." He grinned.

It was finally my turn so I handed everyone their gifts. I thought it was only fair that I spent around $50 on each person just so there wasn't any favoritism or anything. I'd gotten Ashlynn a $50 gift card to Barnes and Noble, a snow board for Jason, the sex positions book and a cock ring for Jade, I got Sarah something blue, which was a single blue cubic zirconia—it looked like a blue diamond—on a necklace for her to wear on her wedding day. I told her she didn't have to wear it if she didn't like it but she started tearing up.

She jumped into my lap and hugged me. I almost thought I was going to die right then and there but she loosened her hold and said, "Thanks, Isabelle," with this huge smile on her face.

As for Gabe, I got him a shirt that read *Sorry, Ladies, but this Sexy Man is TAKEN* along with a book titled *How to Not Fuck Up Your Marriage.*

We hung out with everyone for a little while longer before leaving. I told Ryder I was getting tired because of the alcohol but really I wanted to have a little party of our own. Walking in the door, I gave Ryder a kiss and headed for my room. I heard the television going on in the living room and the fridge opening.

After I closed my bedroom door I got out my Santa outfit and quickly changed into it. The outfit was actually really cute with a short red skirt with white cotton at the edge, a red bra with cotton, and a cute little Santa hat that had glitter all over it. I paired the outfit with thigh high black boots which I'd borrowed from Ashlynn. After curling my hair a little, applying a fresh coat of mascara, and spraying myself with some peppermint perfume, I left my bedroom.

I peeked out and saw Ryder was concentrating on the television and he had a beer in his hand. I walked to the end of the hallway and stood there with a hand on my hip and waited for Ryder to look my way. He was just about to take a sip of his beer when he saw me and his jaw dropped.

I walked over to the television, never taking my eyes off him, and turned it off. He placed the beer on the coffee table and stared at me in amazement. With my arms crossed, I said, "I heard you've been a naughty boy this year Ryder Mitchell." I thought he was going to laugh but he played along with me. "Yes, I have. How are you going to punish me?"

How was I going to punish him? I hadn't actually thought that far ahead. Then an idea came to me and an evil smile came across my face. I lifted my left leg onto the coffee table and he sucked in a breath. He could see that I was commando. He started to get off the couch but I put my hand out in front of him and said, "I'm going to punish you for being so naughty." I waved my hand and gestured for him to sit down. With a frown on his face, he sat back down but never took his eyes off me.

"So Ryder, would you like to tell me why you have been so naughty this year?" He was about to answer me but then his mouth dropped and his eyes got wide. I had never done this before, at least not in front of someone, but I just went with it. I placed my thumb against my clit and started rubbing in circles. I was going torturously slow but I knew if I went faster with Ryder watching, I would come right then and there and I had to keep my head in the game.

I raised an eyebrow. "Fine. If you won't answer that question, then answer this one. What do you want to do to me?"

I saw his Adam's apple move and then he said, "I want to kiss your beautiful lips."

I applied a little more pressure and said, "What else?"

He swallowed again and said, "I want to suck on your nipples."

I added a little more pressure and then pulled down the bra and started pinching and pulling one nipple. Without taking my eyes off him, I said, "What else?"

He moved to the edge of his seat and said, "I want to suck on your clit and put my fingers inside you."

He'd started to get the hang of the game so I rubbed a little harder and then placed a finger inside myself. "What else?"

He moved off the couch and started toward me. "I want you to come harder than you ever have and I want to hear you scream my name."

Without stopping, I whispered, "Make me."

I wasn't even able to finish saying the two words before Ryder lifted me up and slung me on the couch. He ripped off his shirt and then sucked in my lower lip and bit down a little roughly but the pain was a pleasurable one. The second I gasped, he shoved his middle and ring finger inside me and used his thumb to apply pressure to my clit. I wrapped my legs around him and he sucked hard on my nipple and pinched the other one while I played with his hair and sucked on his neck.

I started moving against his fingers and sucked on his earlobe. "Harder." And that's exactly what he did. Ryder added his pointer finger and slightly curved them all the while moving down my body. Before I knew it, he sucked my clit into his mouth and within seconds I was screaming his name over and over again. The second he took his fingers out of me, I was on his lap kissing him.

There was something about tasting myself on him that made me extremely hot. I moved off his body and was kneeling next to him, unbuckling his pants. His cock sprung out in my face and I sucked him into my mouth while squeezing his balls. I was bobbing my head up and down and then I felt a hand in my hair moving it aside and then I felt two fingers push inside of me forcefully. I moaned around his cock and sucked him harder and moved my head up and down faster.

I heard Ryder moaning and saying, "Fuck, Isabelle," over and over again. I felt him getting bigger in my mouth and I knew he was going to come any second. As his sweet liquid squirted in my mouth and his cock twitched, he pushed down roughly on my clit and before I knew it I was coming. My legs quivered. My stomach tightened. My head shook from side to side. My body shook. I gasped for air.

It felt like someone else had taken over my body. I couldn't move even if I wanted to and before I knew it, Ryder lifted me up into his arms and started nuzzling my neck. My mouth was right by his ear. I was still breathing hard. I was trying to form words but then I felt him get hard against my stomach. He could tell that I felt it too because I sucked in a breath and then he put a hand on either side of my face and looked at me. "Sweetheart, when you are breathing uncontrollably like that because of me I get so turned on. Hell, I get turned on just hearing your name."

I still couldn't form simple words so I just kissed him on the lips and nuzzled into him. Ryder lifted me up with him. I thought he was going to take me to my room but he pushed his jeans off. He lay down on the couch with me on his chest and covered us up with a blanket. We both fell into a blissful sleep.

***

The next morning I woke up in Ryder's arms and it was the best feeling in the world. Every time I slept in his arms I got the best night's sleep and I felt safe and warm. I was tracing a finger around his nipple ring when it twitched and I looked up and saw Ryder smiling down at me. "Good morning, beautiful." I smiled and kissed his stomach. "Mmm, yes it is."

He pulled me even closer and then my back was on the couch and he was on top of me. He started to move his head down but I put a hand to his chest to push him off me. "I just have to brush my teeth really quick and then I'll be back."

Ryder put a hand over my wrist and brought it up and around his neck while inching his mouth closer to mine. "I don't care about your morning breath, sweetheart. There's nothing that could keep me away from your sweet little mouth."

I moved my head to the side and then he started nuzzling my neck but pulled back. "Although on second thought, you probably do have really bad morning breath." I turned my head and started to yell at him but his mouth was on mine. He was sucking on my tongue before I could argue with him. I wrapped my arms around him and tilted my head to deepen this kiss and moaned into his mouth.

After a couple minutes of the best make out session ever, he leaned back. He looked at me and then tilted his head to the side. "Yep, maybe you should have brushed your teeth." A huge smile came across his face and then I started laughing at him. He kissed me again on the lips and then started to lift off me.

I sat up. "Where are you going?"

Ryder's back was to me but he turned around and said, "I've got some shopping to do for my beautiful girl today." After he got ready, he kissed me and went on his way. For the rest of the day I just lounged around the house. Sarah and Gabe stopped by before they left for home and told me to have a great holiday. I wrapped Ryder's gifts and then read for a while. I thought he would be home soon but eight hours later he still wasn't home. I thought he would call or text me to let me know he was okay but nothing happened.

I was getting ready for bed and as I reached to turn off my bedroom light, I realized I really missed Ryder. So I walked out of my room and went into his. Even though we were dating, we both needed our space, so we still slept in our own rooms but tonight was different. I went into his room and curled up under his covers. My head was on his pillow and his scent was all around me so that even without him being here physically, I felt safe and drifted off to sleep.

At some point I felt arms wrap around me and Ryder kissed my neck. I turned around in his arms and he was smiling. "I didn't know if this was okay; I can leave if you want your own space." Ryder just chuckled. "This is definitely okay, sweetheart." He leaned down and kissed me on the lips. I thought he was going to deepen the kiss but he simply pulled me closer. I wrapped a leg around his waist and cuddled up. Within seconds we were asleep in one another's arms.

Chapter 14

A week later I woke up to Ryder jumping up and down on my bed. "Merry Christmas, sweetheart!" He looked so gorgeous in the morning. His hair was all over the place, eyes glistening, and a huge smile on his face. "Merry Christmas, Ryd." I jumped up off the bed, grabbed him, and kissed him. I didn't even care that I had morning breath. It didn't matter anymore because nothing could ever stop me from kissing Ryder's lips.

Before he could grab me, I jumped up off the bed and ran to my closet to get his gift. I couldn't wait to see his eyes when he opened it.

Ryder was sitting on my bed just staring at me.

Typical.

I walked up to him and handed him his present. "Here you go." He took it from me and started to rub the back of his neck. "Sweetheart, I feel terrible because I didn't get you anything. I didn't know what exactly to get you so I just thought I could take you shopping. Would that work?"

A normal person would have been devastated.

But I wasn't normal. Far from it, actually.

I couldn't remember the last time I got a present for Christmas.

Or my birthday.

So this was nothing new. I would have been more shocked if he had actually gotten me something.

I put my hand on his shoulder to try and comfort him. "Hey, don't worry about it. You let me stay here for free, so this is the least I could do." He was looking at his present, probably trying to figure out what it was, but then he looked up at me. "Sweetheart, you really don't understand just how much you already do."

Before I could respond he dropped his present on my bed and left my room. I followed after him. "Ryder, what are you doing?" He was searching through his closet for something. "Wait, I might have something you could have in here. How about you just go sit on the bed while I look?" I turned around to sit on the bed and when I turned back around Ryder was standing in front of me with a gift in his hands. I looked at it and then looked up at him. "What's this?"

He started to laugh. "What do you think it is, sweetheart? You really think I'd forget to get my girl something for Christmas?"

I sat down on his bed and whispered, "I just—I didn't expect anything." I didn't know what to do, so I just sat there like an idiot with a stunned look on my face. "Don't just sit there. Open your gift, sweetheart." He pushed the gift into my hands and I looked down at it. The gift was covered in red wrapping paper with Santa Claus in his sleigh and Rudolph and the other reindeers pulling him around. There was gold ribbon wrapped around it and at the top was a bow with a tag attached to it. I read it and almost cried.

To My Sweetheart,
Our first Christmas together, but certainly not our last.
Your Munchkin

I looked at him and bolted out of the room. I could hear him talking to himself in his bedroom and then I heard him kick the wall and march out of his room. "Sweetheart, it's just a gift. You don't have to frea—oof!" He was hunched over and holding his stomach.

My eyes got huge. "I'm sorry. I was just getting you your gift. Are you okay?" Ryder stood up straight and looked at me. "Oh yeah, I'm fine. Come on, I have tattoos and piercings. I'm a motherfucking badass. A little hit in the gut is nothing."

I looked at him and started to chuckle. I could see that my running into him was hurting but he was trying to play it cool. "Okay, well, come on Badass Ryder." I dragged him into the living room and stopped dead in my tracks. "What's all this?"

There were presents everywhere, breakfast was made, and hot chocolate was sitting on the coffee table. Ryder walked in front of me like nothing was different. "It is Christmas, after all." I could feel my eyes starting to mist and a lump forming in my throat. "Why'd you do all of this?" I didn't understand what was going on. This was just so different from anything I had ever experienced or expected.

Ryder was loading a plate up with breakfast items. When he saw that I wasn't standing next to him, he put the plate down and turned around. "I fucked up, didn't I? It's okay, we can do something else. I just really wanted you to enjoy today. That's all." He started clearing off the table and talking to himself when I walked over to him grabbed his arm.

"Ryder, don't do that. I just needed a minute." He was just staring at me, so I proceeded. "Nobody has ever done anything like this for me, so I just needed a minute … or five to take it all in."

"What do you mean, Isabelle? You've never celebrated Christmas?" The look in my eyes must have said it all and before I knew it I was in his arms. He started to rub my back and kissed the top of my head. "Well, you will from now on. You hear me?" He was holding me close so I just nodded. We stood like that for a couple more minutes and then Ryder pushed me back. As he wiped away my tears he said, "All right, enough of this Lifetime shit. Let's get down and dirty in these gifts." He looked at me one more time and the look in his eyes was different.

We walked back over to the breakfast bar and he handed me a plate.

When did he have time to do all of this?

There were eggs, bacon, sausage, hash browns, bagels, and blueberry muffins—my favorite. I put the plate down, grabbed a napkin and a muffin. I started to nibble on it and smiled. I could feel a pair of brown eyes on me and turned to look at Ryder. "What?"

He just laughed. "Really? I make all of this food and you grab a damn muffin. Unbelievable. Well, more for me."

After Ryder got all situated, we walked into the living room and he handed me a hot chocolate. From out of nowhere he pulled out a can of whipped cream and piled it on my drink.

I took a sip of the hot chocolate and realized it was peppermint flavored. I set it down on the coffee table and then heard Ryder gulp. I thought he was choking, so I turned to look at him and he had this weird look on his face. "What?"

Ryder put his plate on the coffee table and the second he turned around, his lips were on mine. I opened my mouth and felt his warm tongue against mine. I started to moan and then Ryder pulled away. It took me a few seconds to catch my breath. When I did, I saw that Ryder had a smirk on his face while he was eating his bagel sandwich. "What was that about? Not that I didn't enjoy it."

Ryder finished the bite that was in his mouth and then swallowed. "You know I have to taste the peppermint hot chocolate. Plus you had whipped cream on your face. We'll definitely have to use that."

Dear Lord,
This is the best Christmas ever!
Amen

I could feel a blush creeping on so I grabbed his gift and handed it to him. He looked down at it and smiled. I had wrapped it in *Wizard of Oz* wrapping paper that had little munchkins all over it.

He started laughing and then looked at me. "Clever, Isabelle. Clever indeed."

I just shrugged my shoulders and smiled. "I thought so."

Ryder put it to the side and got up from the couch and grabbed the gift that he had given to me earlier and set it in my lap. "Merry Christmas, sweetheart." I started to untie the ribbon and noticed that Ryder wasn't opening his gift. I was just about to ask him when he said, "I'll open mine later. I want to see your face when you open your gifts." He took another bite of his sandwich and I began to open my gift. Before all of the paper was off, I knew exactly what it was.

My very own Kindle. I just touched the box and looked it over. I felt my eyes getting watery all over again and I was just about to get the Kindle out of the box when Ryder snatched it from me.

"I will not allow you to open anymore gifts if you're going to cry, sweetheart. You have no idea what your crying does to me."

I quickly wiped my tears away and told him to give it back. I got my Kindle out of the box and started to play around with it. I began downloading free books because I was short on money after getting everybody's gifts. I was just about to get *Pride and Prejudice* when a one – hundred dollar gift card fell into my lap. I picked it up and looked at it and then at Ryder. He pointed to me and warned, "Remember what I said, sweetheart."

I dropped the Kindle onto the couch and lunged at him. He didn't even hesitate and pulled me into his arms while I kissed him. We stayed like that for a few minutes and then I broke our embrace. I pushed him onto the couch and turned around to grab his gift.

"Well, damn, Isabelle. If all I had to do was get you a bunch of gifts to finally have you in my bed, it would've happened months ago." I turned back around and handed him his gift. "Merry Christmas, Ryd." He took the gift from me and for a second just looked at me. I felt like he wanted to say something but he shook his head and started to rip the wrapping paper off.

He sat there for a few minutes just staring at it. I thought maybe I had screwed up and was about to apologize. Then he looked at me and I could see tears in his eyes. He wiped his eyes and started to cough. I wanted to grab him and hold him because seeing him cry wanted to make me cry all over again but for different reasons. I couldn't stand to see Ryder in pain and I couldn't believe that I had caused it. I started to open my mouth but he said, "Isabelle, this is the best gift I have ever been given. Thank you."

I smiled because I was so relieved I hadn't screwed this up. I'd gotten him new tattoo guns, ink, and two plane tickets to Las Vegas. There was a tattoo convention there in April that I'd gotten him tickets to as well. I thought that maybe he and

Gabe could go since they shared the same passion for tattoos.

I was just about to tell him that when he said, "I want you to come with me."

I looked at him. "Where?"

He picked up the plane tickets and waved them in my face. "Here, sweetheart. I want you to come with me."

I pushed his arm away and tried to explain. "Ryder, I know nothing about tattoos. All I know is that they hurt like a bitch. I wouldn't have the full appreciation for it. Besides, I thought you could take Gabe. You guys would have a lot of fun together."

He put the tickets down in his lap and it looked like he was considering it. "Nah, while he would appreciate it, I would appreciate it more if you were there with me. I want you there with me. I want to experience it with you. Plus you'll turn twenty-one while we're there!" I started to laugh again. "Okay, but Ryder, just remember that there are four months until the convention, so just think about it, okay?"

"All right, but my mind is already made up. You're the one I want." The way he said that seemed almost as if he wasn't just talking about me joining him on the trip to Vegas, but I tried not to read too much into it. I felt like things were definitely changing between us. I mean I thought we were just having fun, so I tried to switch the topic. "So what else did you get me, Ryder?"

It seemed almost like he knew that I was trying to change the subject. Instead of calling me on it, he said, "How about you open them and find out?"

Overall I got a pair of UGG boots, some perfume, a Northface jacket with a hat, gloves, and some sweatpants.

For the rest of the day we snuggled on the couch and watched Christmas movies and drank hot chocolate. We were too lazy to actually make a Christmas dinner so we just ordered Chinese food and munched on Chicken and Broccoli, Crab Rangoon, Shrimp Fried Rice, and Spring Rolls.

At one point Ryder turned to me and asked, "So did you get everything you wanted for Christmas?"

I took my eyes off the television to look up at him. "Today was the best. Thank you, Ryd. Did you get everything you wanted?"

He didn't even pause. "All I wanted for Christmas was you." I was about to laugh when I saw that he didn't even blink. There was just something about today that was different. Maybe because Ryder gave me my first Christmas. I started to realize just how much Ryder loved me. I had never experienced most of the things that he had shown me and given me. It wasn't because he had made that Christmas one to remember but I realized in that moment I was in love with Ryder Mitchell. I wanted him in every way.

I had never been straightforward with anything in my life, but Ryder made me feel like I could do or be anything. Infinite. So I grabbed his face and crushed my lips to his. Ryder grabbed a hold of me and pulled me onto his lap without breaking the kiss. He opened his mouth and I gladly opened mine. After a few minutes, he started to kiss my neck down to my collarbone and then made his way back up to my lips. I made my way to the bottom of his shirt and started to pull it up over his head. He could see what I wanted, so he helped me out a little bit. After he dropped the shirt on the floor, he picked me up in his arms and carried me to my room.

Along the way I got rid of my shirt and bra. Before I knew it I was falling on my bed and bringing Ryder along with me. I loved the feel of his skin up against me and I couldn't wait for him to finally be inside me.

He started pinching and pulling a nipple and sucking on my neck. I was sucking on his earlobe when I whispered, "I want you." I thought it was going to turn him on but it did the complete opposite. He jerked his head away and looked at me. I thought his face was going to be filled with desire but he looked ... scared. He got up on his knees and started to rub the back of his neck.

I didn't understand what was going on and then felt really uncomfortable because I was topless. So I sat up and wrapped the blanket around me. I watched him and saw that he was looking down and biting his lip. I just had to know, so I whispered, "Ryder?"

He jerked up to look at me and started rambling. "Isabelle, this isn't what I wanted for today to be. I just wanted you to have a good Christmas and for us to spend time together. I mean, is this what you thought I wanted? Is this what you want? Fuck, I don't want your first time to be like this!"

I felt my eyes watering and I could feel my chin quivering. "Ryder, I don't understand. I thought ..."

"What'd you think? That this is what I wanted?" When I nodded, he said, "No, that's not what I wanted at all."

I could feel tears falling and my heart breaking. I thought he'd wanted me. I thought he'd cared about me, but no. I was stupid enough to believe that someone could actually care about me and not put me down. But I was wrong.

Ryder must have realized what he said and he tried to backtrack. "Isa—" I stood up from the bed and walked over to my closet and yanked a shirt over my head. "Get the fuck out of my room now!"

Ryder just sat there and rubbed his hands together. "Isabelle, that's not what I meant. I mea—"

I looked at him and if looks could kill, Ryder would have been six feet under. "I don't give a fuck what you meant. I don't give a flying fuck anymore. I thought you were different but I was so wrong. You completely played me. You went so far as to introduce me to your family. I thought I was actually falling for you, but you know what I fell for, Ryder? I fell for your bullshit, and guess what? I'm not going to be falling for it anymore. The second I have enough money, I'm out of here. Do you hear me?"

"Swee—"

"Don't you dare *sweetheart* me! Now I know you're not deaf, so I will tell you one more time. Get the fuck out!"

I could see tears forming in his eyes but I didn't care. I thought he'd wanted me. Hell, I'd thought maybe he was falling in love with me. I couldn't

179

believe how stupid I actually was. As soon as I heard the door close behind him, I completely lost it. I grabbed the closest thing to me, which was a framed picture of the two of us, and slammed it against the wall. Then I fell over and bawled.

The glass shattered in the same way my heart shattered at Ryder's words. I knew there was no way I could ever repair that picture frame and I also knew there was no way anybody could ever repair my heart. It was crushed.

I finally managed to stop crying and just fell on my bed. I didn't change. I didn't wrap myself up in my blanket. I just felt numb and stared at the wall. Before I knew it my eyelids were shutting and I was thinking that Christmas was the worst holiday ever.

Chapter 15

The next morning my head was killing me. I wished it was a bad dream and that I'd woken up in the comfort of Ryder's arms, but it wasn't. This was my reality and I had to face it and move on.

After getting ready, I walked out into the living room to get my shoes and jacket. I was prepared to start my apartment hunting today because I couldn't live with Ryder any longer. I started past the breakfast bar when I saw Ryder's back was to me and he was busy making breakfast. There were two plates set out with orange juice and coffee next to them. Ryder had to be fucking kidding himself if he thought that was an apology. He must have heard me walk out because he turned around with a small smile on his face.

I couldn't believe the bastard was actually smiling. He'd broken my heart yet had the nerve to think that making scrambled eggs and toast was going to make everything better.

He must have seen the pissed off look on my face because his smile turned to a thin line. "Isabelle, I want to apologize."

I thought I'd gotten all of my tears and frustration out last night but apparently not. "I don't want to hear it, Ryder. I just can't believe I fell for your bullshit. I can't believe I actually wanted you to be my first. You completely played me, and after everything that I told you about Cynthia." I huffed and puffed and felt tears in my eyes. I thought blinking a few times would make them go away but when I opened my eyes, they fell down my face. "But I guess Cynthia was right. I am stupid and nobody will ever care about me."

Ryder started toward me but I put my hand up. "Don't. If I could, I would leave today but I don't have enough money to go anywhere. Until I do move out, I'll pay half of the rent and whatever else I need to pay for." Since all I did was save my money since Ryder didn't allow me to pay for rent or anything I was able to buy all those gifts. But now I was broke because I may have gone a little overboard. I just didn't calculate into it that Ryder and I would be breaking up and I would need to move out. I looked in the direction of the gifts, waved my hands and said, "You can keep the gifts because I don't want them."

He started to open his mouth again but I beat him to it. "I don't want to hear it, Ryder. I thought you were different but last night put everything into perspective for me."

With that I left the apartment and began my search for an apartment and another job. I knew just working at the library wouldn't make me enough money to move out anytime soon so I drove around and put in applications. I was just about to give up my search when I was at a red light and saw a *Now Hiring* sign in front of a local bookstore. As soon as the light turned green, I pulled up in front of the bookstore and parked.

I walked into the store and a jingle went off. Somebody from the back came out in front. "Hi. How can I help you?" The guy seemed really sweet. He had brown wavy hair and was tall and lean. He was wearing skinny blue jeans with a red sweatshirt and black framed glasses.

I smiled and said, "I saw that you were hiring."

He started jumping up and down and squealing at the top of his lungs. "Oh, thank God. I thought I was going to die here without any help." He must have seen the scared look on my face because he walked out from behind the counter and said, "I'm Patrick Christiansen."

I put my hand out. "I'm Isabelle." He looked down at my hand and tilted his head to the side. Instead of shaking my hand he laughed and pulled me into a huge hug. I should have been shocked that this complete stranger hugged me but there was something about him that was really comfortable.

Instead of pulling away from me completely, he wrapped an arm around me and started to walk me into the back. "Come on, I'll show you around." Patrick was really nice. He showed me all that I had to do, which wasn't all that much. I just had to keep everything organized, help the customers out if they had any questions, and ring them out. He told me the hardest part was to have to keep a smile plastered on your face because some of the customers could be real "Bitch Skanks" as he put it.

***

For the rest of break Ryder and I stayed away from one another. I thought it was going to be pretty difficult but Ryder decided to go home. A couple of times Sarah called me and tried to get me to explain what had actually happened between us. She informed me that Ryder was taking it pretty badly but I didn't care. I told her that what happened was between Ryder and me and if he wanted to explain it to her, then he could.

I was done giving a shit. While my heart was broken I wasn't going to talk a bunch of shit on him. After all he gave me a place to sleep and put food in my stomach when he really didn't have to, so I just let it go. I was just happy that I didn't really have time to think about it. School was going to be starting up again soon and I had two jobs to keep me plenty busy.

Working at my new job was pretty awesome. Patrick was hilarious and in my spare time I got to read a bunch of the books we sold. I also got to read *The Sea of Tranquility* and told Patrick he had to read it. He told me that he loved it. He also told me he loved that I worked there with him. While I helped out the customers he was able to get the background work done a lot faster. When I wondered why he was the only person who worked there he told me that his grandparents owned it. He said that they joked around that it didn't take a rocket scientist to work at a bookstore so they let Patrick work there.

He told me that this time of the season was pretty dead, so while I sat on my stool in front of the store and read, Patrick was working in the back. I was at a good part in my book when the jingle went off, informing me that somebody walked in. I bookmarked my page and looked up to see it was the guy from Spencer's who had hit on me. He looked up and smiled when he recognized me. "Hey."

I smiled and waved at him. Without taking his eyes off me, he walked right in front of me and smiled. "So how'd the boyfriend like the outfit?"

My smile instantly disappeared and I said, "Oh, um, we broke up."

His smile also disappeared but then a cocky grin took its place. "That's a damn shame because I know without a doubt you would have looked real sexy in that outfit." I could feel a blush on my face but I shook my head.

I looked up and saw he was still smiling. "So, I was thinking since you guys broke up, how about I take you out for some coffee or something?" he asked.

I was taken off guard. "I'm still getting over the break up but maybe some other time?"

I could tell that my answer wasn't the one he was hoping for but he smiled again. "Well, it wasn't a *no,* so maybe I'll see you around, Isabelle." With that he turned around and started to walk out of the store. I was just about to ask him to tell me his name again but he turned around and said, "It's Neil James, by the way. Just in case you forgot."

After the door closed behind him I heard, "Damn, that's a fine ass." I turned to see Patrick staring in Neil's direction and started laughing. He looked at me and said, "Oh honey, I'm gay. I thought you knew?"

"I had my suspicions but I wanted to wait for you to tell me." He smiled and then completely switched topics. "So you just broke up with your boyfriend?" I told Patrick I didn't really feel like talking about it. Patrick assured me he was a great listener and that he would be there whenever I wanted to talk about it. He was just about to walk in the back and get back to work when I spilled everything.

I told him about how Ryder and I were first friends and I moved in with him because of the whole financial aid fiasco and how things started changing. I told him about how he'd introduced me to his family and gave me a tattoo. I also told him about the last night we were together and how I was ready to give up my virginity but he rejected me.

I cried and it took a while for me to get everything out but after I finished, Patrick pulled me into his arms and whispered, "Oh honey, he's a jackass. I think he's just as scared as you. But I do have a solution to your problem."

He was still playing with my hair when I said, "What?"

Patrick put me at arm's length and said, "My roommate just moved to California so I have a room available. Keep in mind that it's not big or anything, but it's a roof over your head and it's dirt cheap. Plus my grandparents live next door and they're awesome. My grandma makes the best apple walnut waffles ever and my grandpa is fucking hysterical. I'm not saying you have to, but it's an option if you want."

I wrapped my arms around his neck and kissed him on the cheek. "Thanks, Patrick." I pulled away and looked at him. "You're amazing. You know that, right?"

He just shrugged his shoulders and said, "Sweetie, I'm fucking awesome!" I had no words so I just laughed and we got back to work.

***

It was two months into the new semester and Ryder and I were getting along better. He and I both worked a lot and were rarely ever home at the same time so it was really easy to stay away from each other. At first it was hard on everyone but I told them that I didn't want sides to be taken. Ryder and I had made our decision so that was all there was to it. Sarah and Gabe didn't agree with us breaking up but decided to let it go.

Jade gave a sneaky smile when we all asked her about the cock ring and said, "That's for me to know, bitches, and for you to find out!" Jason ended up breaking up with Christie over break and Ashlynn "broke up" with Derrick as well. I told her that it was a good decision and she realized that it was for the best and she was ready to move on with her life. She also told me that Derrick was fine with the "breaking up." He told her that he was tired of pretending and whether people liked it or not, he was going to live his life the way he wanted to. No more hiding.

It was a Saturday night and we all decided to have a girl's night out, which consisted of Sarah, Jade, Ashlynn, Derrick, Patrick and I. In a drunken state, Ashlynn told everyone that she and Derrick dating was just to get Jason jealous.

We all laughed and Jade said, "I can't believe I'm related to a dumbass!" While we all needed a night out to just relax because of our hectic schedules, I had secret motives. I thought Derrick and Patrick would be really cute together. While Derrick was a little quiet, Patrick was loud and flamboyant and told you to your face exactly how it was.

After we all ordered our drinks we went onto the dance floor. I had my arms wrapped around Patrick and we were laughing and having a good time. When the song was over we walked back over to the bar and ordered shots of tequila for everyone and while we waited, I started up *Operation: Get Patrick and Derrick together.*

I was just about to open my mouth when Patrick turned to me with a huge smile plastered to his face. After taking a sip of my beer I said, "What are you smiling about, cutiepie?"

"Besides the fact that Derrick is completely cute and totally fuckable?"

I giggled and said, "I thought you guys would be really cute together. I mean, you guys look totally adorable together but you also even each other out really well."

He smiled again and hugged me. "I completely love you, gorgeous, but that's not why I'm smiling." I pulled out of his embrace and had *confused* written all over my face.

He moved closer to me and said, "That hottie from the bookstore is here and he hasn't taken his eyes off you since we walked in." My eyes bugged out of my head and I turned around. Neil was on the other side of the bar drinking a beer and looking directly at me. I spun right around and Patrick started giggling. I was about to ask him what I should do when the bartender placed the tequila shots in front of us and Patrick handed me one. "You might need this because hottie is walking over here right now!" I took the shot back and welcomed the warm liquid and then sucked on the lime.

As soon as I turned around, Neil was right in front of me. He didn't say anything. Just placed a hand in front of me and said, "Dance with me." I put my hand in his and Neil walked me out onto the dance floor. I could see out of the corner of my eye that Sarah, Jade, Ashlynn, and Derrick were watching me but I didn't care.

As soon as we were in the middle of the dance floor I wrapped my arms around his neck and Neil wrapped his arms around my waist. I was grateful that a slow song was playing because I was a little nervous. We danced for a few minutes then Neil said, "So about that date?"

I smiled against his chest and lifted my head to look up into his eyes. I huffed and said, "I really appreciate it but I'm just not ready yet. For now I just want to be single and have fun in college."

He shrugged his shoulders and said, "It was worth a shot, but whoever you end up with is going to be real lucky."

I kissed him on the cheek and said, "Thank you." We danced a few more songs and then went our separate ways.

Neil was really cute but I just wasn't ready to go into another relationship so fast. A part of me was still hoping there was a chance with Ryder. There was just something that stuck out to me. When Ryder and I first broke up, I thought he was going to go back to his old ways of just having sex with girls but he did the exact opposite. He started working all of the time and I wondered if maybe he did actually care about me and I had made a horrible mistake. I started second guessing myself and questioning my motives but I realized that if I had make a mistake, Ryder would have tried to convince me otherwise. He didn't do that. He just kind of dropped it and let it go and that hurt more than words could ever describe.

Memo to the Male Species:

Girls like men who know what they want and go after it, not boys who twiddle their thumbs and make it a puzzle we girls have to solve. Because guys, we aren't going to solve that riddle. Hate to break it to ya!

I decided right then and there that I needed to move on with my life and not hold out for something that could possibly never happen. I noticed Patrick and Derrick were talking over at the bar and while I didn't want to interrupt, I knew that if I didn't go over there I would psych myself out. I walked over to the bar, wrapped my arms around Patrick from behind, and kissed him on the cheek.

"Is that room still available?" Patrick swung around and picked me up and started cheering. "Hell, yeah, it is, gorgeous! OMG, we are going to have so much fun. We can eat ice cream and watch a bunch of chick flicks and—"

As much as I wanted to talk about being roommates with Patrick, I wanted Patrick and Derrick to continue talking more so I said, "We can talk about this later, cutiepie." I kissed him on the cheek and walked over to where Sarah, Jade, and Ashlynn were dancing.

We all started dancing together and I looked over in the direction of Patrick and Derrick and smiled, because as I came to the realization that Ryder and I would never be, another relationship was beginning to blossom. With some water, sunlight, and a lot of patience, it would become a beautiful thing.

Chapter 16

Ryder and I rarely saw each other but on one of the rare occasions we did, I told him that I was moving out. He didn't say anything, just shrugged his shoulders and went into his room. Part of me felt like complete shit because I couldn't believe that this was how it was going to end, but I knew he'd deserved to be told in person. He didn't deserve a text that read:

Me: I'm moving out.

Patrick and I talked all the time and he couldn't wait for me to move in with him. It had been three weeks since our girls' night out and Patrick and Derrick were still dating. They seemed really happy together and I was extremely happy for the both of them. Derrick had gone through a lot and didn't deserve the hatred of others putting him down and hiding who he truly was and I was so happy that he'd found Patrick. Patrick introduced Derrick to his grandparents and they instantly loved him.

Derrick had worried if it was too early but Patrick said, "Why stop the inevitable?"

I had wanted to move into Patrick's sooner but my course load and working two jobs was taking up all of my time. When I wasn't working, I was either doing homework or going to classes. When I finally had a weekend off, I decided to buckle down and get a move on. I got all of the boxes, duct tape, and markers that I would need and began to pack up my room.

I was folding clothes and putting them in boxes, wrapping up picture frames filled with my friends and Ryder. I was playing music but I heard slamming coming from the kitchen and glass shattering, so I got up off the floor and walked over to my door. I didn't think Ryder was going to be here but apparently he was. A part of me didn't want to see what all of the noise was but I turned the knob and walked out anyway.

I stopped at the bathroom and heard more things breaking and deep breathing in and out. I took a deep breath and walked out into the living room and turned to look at the kitchen. It took me a second to comprehend what exactly was going on. Ryder was holding a beer in one hand and grabbing anything breakable in the other and throwing it at the wall as hard as he possibly could.

"What the hell is the matter with you? Why are you acting like this?" I screamed. He dropped the plate he was holding and it crashed to the floor below him, then he turned to look at me. I had never seen this side of Ryder before. His eyes were filled with so much anger and rage that it scared me a little. I started to back up and I could see in his eyes that he realized he was scaring me. He put down his beer and took a deep breath before he opened his mouth. "Why are you doing this?"

Was he serious? He was the one throwing dishes against the wall and shattering them. I was just packing up my room. There was no contest.

"Because I can't deal with *this* anymore. What we have going on between us. Hell, I don't even know what it is. You introduce me to your family over Thanksgiving break. You surprise me on Christmas Day. You gave me the best Christmas ever and then that same night you took it all away. You rejected me and it crushed my heart. I thought for a second you actually cared about me but Cynthia was right. I am stupid."

He picked the beer back up off the counter and took a healthy gulp. "You belong in a fucking psych ward if you truly think that!"

I laughed at him. "Which part, exactly? The part where you rejected me? The part where I think I'm stupid? Please, Ryder, tell me exactly which part you're talking about?" He slammed the beer he was holding up against the wall and it splattered everywhere. Foam started running down the wall onto the carpet.

"Dammit, you are the dumbest, most stubborn person I have ever met in my entire life!" I couldn't believe how angry he was getting. Veins were bulging out of his neck and for a second I thought he was going to turn into the Incredible Hulk.

If anyone was supposed to be mad it should have been me. The one person I thought I trusted was telling me exactly what I already knew. "See? Even you think it!" I screamed back.

In an instant Ryder lunged at me and grabbed me by the arms. He was squeezing so hard that he was going to leave bruises. He could see in my eyes I was in pain and he loosened his hold on me. "Fuck, Isabelle. I also think you are the smartest, most beautiful girl I have ever met and if you pulled your head out of your ass and opened your eyes for two fucking seconds, you would see that I love you."

I almost didn't hear him but I had never had anybody say those words to me before. "Y-you what?" I could feel the tears starting to form in my eyes, but I wouldn't allow Ryder to see me cry about him anymore. I wouldn't allow anymore tears to fall because of him. For him.

He let go of me and started backing up into the breakfast bar. "You heard me. From the moment I saw you it has always been you. It will always be just you."

I couldn't take this bullshit anymore. One minute he was pushing me away and just as fast he was pulling me back. Shit. Even right now he was saying these beautiful words and all the while he was walking away from me. But I couldn't let the words *I love you* leave my head. Nobody had ever said those words to me before. Until now.

"Ryder Tyler Mitchell, don't you dare say things like that to me if you don't mean it." He sat down on a stool and slammed his fist on the breakfast bar. For a second I thought the top was going to crack. "Now why the hell not? It's the goddamn motherfucking truth!" I thought I had calmed him down, but apparently not.

But I was so extremely tired of this bullshit. We had been playing this back and forth game for so long and I didn't think I could take it any longer. Someone can only drag you around for so long and then you get tired. So extremely tired of being dragged around in the horseshit that you just cut ties with them. This was my final straw and I was holding the scissors, prepared to cut my ties. So I decided to hell with it. I decided to just put all of my feelings out there and see where it took me. Without taking my eyes off him, I said with as much conviction as possible, "Because you are the one person in this fucked up world I actually believe and because you're starting to steal my heart."

I think he was just as shocked as I was to hear those words fall from my mouth, but just as fast, he shook his head back and forth and started chuckling. Then he stopped, looked me straight in the eyes and turned completely serious. "Well, good. It's about damn time, Isabelle, because you stole my heart months ago."

I didn't have time to think, let alone react, because he grabbed me and crushed his mouth to mine. He lifted me up onto the breakfast bar without breaking the kiss and I wrapped my arms and legs around him. He was holding me as if I was going to disappear at any moment. As if what was happening between us right now wasn't real. I could relate.

Before I knew it I was collapsing onto his bed. Then I realized it was my bed. I looked up into his eyes with a curious look. It was almost as if he could read my mind because he said, "That's where all the other girls were. I don't want that for you. You deserve so much better than that. Than me."

In a weird way I found that romantic. I didn't want to think about the others. What mattered was that right now it was me and Ryder. No one else mattered in my opinion. I put my hands to the bottom of his shirt and I felt him jerk against me.

He put his hands over mine to stop me. "Are you sure, Isabelle? Because I can wait as long as you need."

I looked up into his eyes. Eyes that were filled with longing and desire. I felt the butterflies fluttering in my stomach and the wetness pooling between my legs. I thought we were over months ago, but I was wrong. We had never really been apart and I thought back to Christmas when I thought I was ready to have sex with Ryder. I knew it would have been amazing but I would have missed out on the words he'd just said and in that moment I knew. "Maybe you can wait but I can't. Please, Ryder. Make love to me."

That's all it took because Ryder crushed his mouth to mine and pushed his tongue in. He slowly pushed me back onto the bed and I could feel just how badly he wanted me through his sweat pants. That turned my light switch on and I went crazy. Sex crazy. I pushed him off me so he was lying on his back and I put a leg over him so I was straddling him. I went crazy on his mouth and then I started to move down his body.

I stopped at his nipple rings and started to flick one with my tongue while one of my hands went in his sweatpants and took ahold of him. I started to move my hand up and down and started to swirl my tongue around his nipple. "Sweetheart, you really don't have to do th—ah fuck!" Just before he was about to finish in my hands he grabbed ahold of me by the hips and pulled me up so we were at eye level. In this deep sexy voice he said, "Isabelle, when I come it's going to be inside you."

Fuck, that's hot!

Within a second he jumped off the bed and ran into his room. I heard some banging around and the next thing I knew he was standing in my doorway leaning against it with his arms crossed over his bare, chiseled chest. I thought for a moment he was going to change his mind and let me down. Again. But he smiled at me and said, "You're beautiful, Isabelle."

My heart swelled and we stared at one another for a few moments and then Ryder approached the bed. My bed. I was sitting up on my elbow, drinking him in. He stopped right in front of me, pushing his sweatpants down his body but leaving his boxers on. He was breathtaking. I sat up and let my legs dangle on either side of him. He rested his hands at the middle point of my thighs and waited. It was almost as if he wanted to see what I was going to do.

He was giving me permission to do what I wanted. So I touched him. I touched his abs. His nipple rings. His arms, which were covered with tattoos. His face. I touched his lips. His dimples.

His nose. His ears. I was going to memorize his entire body so I would never forget tonight and how he felt up against me. In me.

I could feel Ryder's eyes on me the whole time I touched him and could feel his breath against my face. I didn't look in his eyes the entire time and then I cradled his face in mine and looked up at him. I was still in shock. Not because I was about to have sex, but because it was going to be with Ryder.

I smiled up at him and pulled his head down to mine so he would kiss me. The kiss was like none we had ever had before. Most of our kisses were wild and crazy. But not this one. This one meant something so much more.

We could have kissed for five minutes or five hours and I would have never known the difference. Ryder started to kiss down my neck and his hands made their way to the bottom of my t-shirt. He pulled back to look into my eyes, asking for my permission. I couldn't form words so I just nodded. He pulled the shirt up and over my head and then moved his hands to my back to unclasp my bra. His fingers never left my body when he took the bra off and let it fall to the floor.

"Lie down on the bed, Isabelle." I looked up into his eyes and they were filled with such hunger that I gulped and did as he said. My head hit the pillow and I turned to look up at him. He was looking down at me and smiling. He walked to the edge of the bed and his fingers started at my toes and he lightly grazed his way up to my stomach without taking his eyes off mine. It was almost as if he were drinking me in, memorizing me, too. Memorizing my touch, my taste.

For a while he just stood there and a million thoughts were running through my mind. I felt like my heart was beating out of my chest and my lungs couldn't get enough oxygen. It felt like all of the air had escaped my bedroom and that I was living on borrowed time. Tick-tock. Tick-tock. I thought I was going to pass out or fall over dead. Then I looked into Ryder's eyes and I felt like everything was going to be okay. That this huge weight had been lifted off my shoulders. That for the first time in my life I could finally breathe and with his help I could get through anything. I just had one question for him to answer.

One question that I had literally been running from. But at this moment, here in this room, I felt brave enough to finally ask the question I had been dying to know the answer to for months now.

I felt like it was a now or never moment, a pass or fail. I felt like in life we are given a test and this one was mine. That if I didn't ask the question I would suffocate and regret it for the rest of my life.

But now, lying here, I realized that it didn't matter what the answer was. What mattered was that I had been brave enough to finally ask it. That I had put my heart out on the line and that maybe, just maybe Ryder could show me that not everybody is like Cynthia. Just one question.

"What do you want from me, Ryder?"

Without taking his eyes off me, he put his hand to my cheek and said, "Everything, Isabelle. Everything." And then he was on the bed lying between my legs, looking into my eyes, and what I saw wasn't lust, but love. Of course a tear escaped my eyes and he reached up to wipe it away.

He sat back on his knees and it looked like he had been run over by a truck. His chest was heaving up and down he was breathing so fast. He lowered his head and I sat up and put my hand under his chin so he would look at me. I saw that his eyes were beginning to well up with tears. I put my hand to his cheek and asked him what was wrong. "Isabelle, we don't have to do this. I don't want you to regret it. Regret me." His voice was filled with so much sorrow. How could he possibly think that I didn't want him? At that moment I finally realized I was deeply and irrevocably in love with Ryder Tyler Mitchell. There was no one else for me because I was taken. Ryder was it and he always would be.

I put my hand to his heart and could feel it beating rapidly. "I love you, Ryder." His heartbeat slowed down to a regular tempo and his breathing was back to normal.

He bent his head and smiled at me. "You have no idea how long I have waited to hear those words come from your beautiful lips." And then he gave me the lightest kiss known to mankind. It was so sweet, yet so passionate all at the same time.

He pushed me back so I was lying on the bed and then his hands were at the top of my shorts. He began to slide them down and I lifted my hips so they would come off more easily. I didn't realize that he had taken my panties off as well until they were at my knees. Ryder dropped both of them off the end of the bed and then he was up off the bed. He put his hands at the top of his boxers and slid them down, never taking his eyes off mine. He then turned and walked over to my dresser and grabbed the condom that he'd put there earlier. He climbed back on the bed, kneeling between my legs. He put the wrapper to his teeth and ripped it open, taking the condom out and sliding it over him.

I couldn't wait for the next time so I could put the condom on him.

He lay down on top of me and I could feel his head at my entrance. He put a hand on each side of my face and said, "I'm going to try and go really slow, Isabelle." I opened my legs up wider and wrapped them around him. He started to slide into me and I closed my eyes.

The instant I closed my eyes he stopped and I opened my eyes. "What's wrong, Ryder?"

He kissed my lips and said, "I want you to look at me." I nodded and he began to push into me further. I kept my eyes open but I winced when he got to a certain point. He immediately stopped. "Are you okay?" I closed my eyes and started to take slow, even breaths. After a few seconds, I opened my eyes and nodded, and then he took a deep breath and pushed all the way in.

After twenty years I had finally given my gift away to Ryder and he had accepted it. I knew that he would cherish it.

He let out a breath I didn't realize he was holding and then he started to suck and kiss my neck. He was letting me get used to his length and boy, did I need to get used to it. I felt full. More than full. Ryder made me feel full. But before long, I was ready to move, so I lifted my hips and heard Ryder hiss through his teeth. I thought maybe I hurt him but he said, "Isabelle, I'm about to come. You've got to warn me when you start to do that. Okay, sweetheart?"

At first I thought it was a joke but I could see the seriousness in his face and hear it in his voice. I couldn't help giggling and then I nodded my head. I couldn't believe that I held so much power over this man and it really turned me on.

He quirked his eyebrows at me. "Oh, you think that's funny, sweetheart?" He started to tickle me and it made me move against him harder, which made him stop the tickle attack altogether.

I put my hands to his face and whispered, "Please, Ryder."

He started off slow and then he sped up and I met him thrust for thrust. There was sweat forming at the top of his forehead and I could feel sweat droplets on his lower back where my hands were. I started to close my eyes because I knew I was close and it was becoming too much to handle. Ryder slowed down and I quickly opened my eyes. "Keep your eyes open, sweetheart." He started to speed up again and before I knew it we were both coming together. I was pulsating around him and I knew from the look on his face and the way he said *Isabelle* that he was filling up his condom.

As good as it felt with him inside me, I started to wonder what it would feel like without the condom. Skin on skin. His skin in my skin. I wanted to know exactly what it would feel like when he came in me.

We didn't last long because of the anticipation of us being together. Just before we both finished, I whispered in his ear, "*I love you.*"

Chapter 17

I woke up the next morning and started to move around. Shit, was I sore. I didn't even know half of those muscles existed until last night. Then I remembered last night and how amazingly wonderful it was. I brushed my fingers against my lips and started to smile.

I started remembering the words.

Every touch.

Every taste.

Every noise.

I rolled over to the side and saw Ryder's head was propped up in his hand and he was watching me. He had this dazed look on his face and I wondered if the same memories were running through his mind. I wrapped my hands around him and kissed him. When I leaned back to look in his face, his eyebrows were scrunched together and he was biting his lower lip.

I didn't understand what was going on. I thought he would pounce all over me but it was the exact opposite. He was treating me like a piece of glass and he was afraid he was going to break me. I cupped his cheek and began to move my thumb over his bottom lip. "Ryder?"

He wrapped a hand around my wrist and kissed the inside of my hand. I saw him close his eyes and then he took a deep breath. Without looking at me he said, "Do you regret what happened last night?"

I didn't understand where this was coming from. I moved up on my elbows so my face was directly aligned with his and kissed him. I pulled away and started to giggle. "Not one bit, silly." I then turned completely serious and cupped his face in my hands and looked directly into his eyes. "I love you, Ryder. That will never change."

He smiled his beautiful smile and kissed me back but pulled away again. "Are we getting back together?"

I bit my lip and shrugged my shoulders and gave him my smartass answer. "I mean, I guess, since I love you and all. You know?" He started laughing and kissed me again but pulled back. *Okay, seriously, I'm getting really pissed off. Shut up, Ryder, and kiss me already!*

I looked at him and raised my eyebrows and he laughed again. "Okay, one more, sweetheart. Are you still moving out?" My smile disappeared. I knew after last night and everything that had happened that I wouldn't be moving out but I didn't want to crush Patrick. He was so excited and we had been planning all these things that we would have been doing, but Ryder was more important because in the simplest of ways *I was totally, completely, hopelessly, endlessly in love with him.*

I could see he was starting to get nervous because I didn't answer right away and I began to giggle. I saw his frown quickly disappear, to be replaced with a cocky grin. He started laughing and then began to tickle me. "You are such a little tease!"

I started laughing really loudly and before I knew it he had both of my arms over my head. "Surrender."

I shook my head back and forth. "Never." He looked at me and this mischievous smile came across his face which made me a little nervous. Deliciously nervous.

He moved his head so his lips were barely grazing mine and he whispered in a sexy low moan, "Oh, I will convince you, sweetheart." He still had my hands pinned above my head when he started to move down my body and suck, kiss, and lick his way to where he knew I would be ready for him. He let go of my hands but lifted his head. "Keep your hands above your head, sweetheart." Shakily, I moved my hands back above my head and held onto the headboard. I wanted to touch him but this experience was definitely going to be one I would always remember.

I felt him smile against my belly button and then he groaned. "Open your legs up wide, sweetheart." I obeyed and he moved down lower and I felt the vibrations of his moan against me. He moved my lips apart and blew cool air on my clit and I got goose bumps all over the place. I started to move my hips up because I needed the release but Ryder said, "Stay still, sweetheart."

With all of my willpower I lowered my hips and heard him chuckle. I looked down at him and saw that he was watching me. He could clearly see that I was getting annoyed and I said, "Bastard."

His lips twitched and before I knew it he was licking me, sucking me, and flicking me with his tongue. He was going crazy and he buried his face in me. I felt the beginnings of a powerful orgasm building up when Ryder stopped abruptly and moved up my body.

I was about to protest and tell him to keep going but he ripped a condom open with his teeth and as soon as he had it on, he slid right inside me. I started to unwind my hands from the headboard but Ryder stopped and said, "Keep your hands up there, sweetheart." Sadly, I obliged, and he kept going. He was moving at a deliriously slow pace that just pissed me off so I wrapped my legs around him for him to go deeper.

He smirked at me. "You want me to go faster?" I looked at him and realized there was something going on with the way he was acting. "Yes, Ryder." He chuckled. "Do you surrender?"

Oh, you have got to be shitting me? Really? That motherfucker thinks he's going to get me to surrender just with his body? Never!

My face must have given him his answer because he started to swivel his hips. *Okay, maybe he might just change my mind. Oh, who am I kidding?*

"Surrender yet?" I couldn't form words so I just shook my head back and forth and moaned something incoherently. Ryder started to pull out and I was about to protest but he slammed right into me.

I screamed, "Yes, Ryder!"

He pulled out of me again and said, "I need to hear you say it, Isabelle."

Before I opened my mouth he slammed into me again and I screamed my answer. "Yes, Ryder, I surrender. Just fuck me already!"

I didn't even get to finish saying *already*, because he was pulling out so just the tip was inside and he was slamming right into me. He had an arm by my head and the other was wrapped around my wrists at the post of the bed. After that no words were said. Just the bed creaking, moaning, and grunting coming from both of us and our bodies slapping together.

I felt the beginnings of an orgasm when Ryder said, "Isabelle?" I bit my lip and shook my head back and forth. Before I knew it the hand that was wrapped around my wrists traveled down my body and as soon as his thumb rubbed against my clit I started to spasm and shake. He pushed into me two more times and then stilled.

He was still rubbing my clit, drawing out my orgasm as long as he could. I thought I was going to die from how strong it was. I screamed, "Ryder!" over and over and over again.

When my body started to come down from the high I closed my eyes and tried to control my breathing. I heard Ryder chuckling and my eyes opened. He was looking down at me with this huge smile on his face.

I laughed and shook my head back and forth. "You are such a bastard. You know that, right?" He laughed louder this time and his body started shaking. I pushed him off me and as soon as his back hit the mattress, I was on top of him, pushing his arms over his head. The image was actually really pathetic because if he wanted to, Ryder could have broken me in half. He was looking up at me with such love and care in his eyes, though. It made me smile even more and right before I kissed him on the lips, I said, "But you're my bastard and I love you."

Ryder wrapped his arms around me and then spun us so I was lying on my back. I started to move my head up to kiss him but he backed away and got up off the bed. "This is just how I want you when I get back," and with that he put on some boxers and walked out of the room.

I bit my lip and smiled to myself because I couldn't believe how quickly things had changed within the last twenty-four hours. When I woke up yesterday, I never thought that today I would be naked in bed with Ryder, laughing and giggling. I started to look around my room and saw all of the boxes. I had totally forgotten about moving in with Patrick. I quickly got up off the bed, and before I used the restroom, I put on Ryder's t-shirt from last night. I couldn't help but sniff the collar because it reminded me of him and his scent steadied my crazy nerves. The cologne mixed with his scent was my undoing.

After using the bathroom, I grabbed my phone from the nightstand. My heart was beating so fast but I knew I had to have this conversation. I scrolled through my contacts and stopped on Patrick's name. Before I could psych myself out, I hit his name and I lifted the phone to my ear as it began to ring. I thought it was going to go to voicemail but I heard, "Hello?"

"Hey, Patr—"

"Oh hey, gorgeous. What's going on?"

My heart was beating out of my chest and Patrick must have realized something was wrong because he said, "What's the matter?" I closed my eyes and took a deep breath. "Ryder and I got back together." I heard squealing and cheering coming from the other end and I started to smile. Between the clapping and yelling Patrick said, "So what's the matter, gorgeous? I thought this was supposed to be a good thing?"

I began to pick my nails. "It is …"

"But …?" There were a few seconds of silence and then I said, "But that means I can't move in with you." There was silence for a long time and I looked at my phone to see if maybe Patrick had hung up on me but I saw that the call was still going through. "Hello?"

I heard sniffling on the other end and could feel tears welling up in my eyes. "Patrick, I'm so sorry. I can still move in with you if you wa—"

"Absolutely not, Isabelle! I'm so happy for you guys. Don't you dare move in with me because I won't allow it. You understand me, gorgeous?"

"But then why are you crying?"

He started to laugh and said, "It's stupid, really. It's just I can't believe how much you care about me. I mean, I had my grandparents, and then I met you, and oh, I just love you, Isabelle. You will always be my best girlfriend. But as your bestest friend in the whole wide world, it is my duty to not let you move in with me. However, I do expect girl nights at least once a week with wine and gossip and ice cream. Oh, and chick flicks!"

I started to giggle and wiped the few remaining tears off my face. "I wouldn't have it any other way!" There was another silence and then I said, "I love you too, Patrick." Even though I wasn't having this conversation with him face to face, I knew he was smiling on the other side of the phone.

"Gorgeous, I'll let you go but I want to see your face ASAP."

"Just name the time and place, cutiepie, and I'll be there."

As soon as I hung up the phone, Ryder walked back into my bedroom wearing his boxers really low and carrying a tray filled with breakfast items. I had a smile on my face by the time the conversation ended with Patrick but my smile grew even wider when I saw Ryder.

He leaned into the doorway and looked at me and a little smile came across his face. "What, sweetheart?"

I just shrugged my shoulders. "You." He smiled and approached the bed. He handed me the tray and then climbed on and sat across from me. I looked down at the tray and saw some coffee and bagels with cream cheese. After picking up my cup and taking a sip, I said, "Thank you. This is wonderful."

Swallowing his bite of bagel and cream cheese, he said, "It's just coffee and bagels, sweetheart."

My mouth twitched. Looking over at him I said, "Yeah, but you thought about me when you made it. *That,* Ryder, is what makes it so wonderful."

With his bagel still in hand, he leaned over and kissed me on the lips. He kissed me a few more times and as he pulled away he said, "I love you, Isabelle." I moved my head in and kissed him one more time. Against his lips, I said, "I love you too, Ryder."

We drank our coffee and ate our bagels while making mindless conversation. After we were done, Ryder put the tray on the floor and cuddled up next to me. He rubbed my back while I swirled circles along his stomach with my fingers.

We laid there in a comfortable silence but then Ryder said, "Will you still come to the tattoo convention with me, sweetheart?"

I lifted my head and smiled. "Of course I will, if that's what you want."

He wrapped me in his arms and pulled me closer. "That's exactly what I want, Isabelle." I kissed his neck and said, "I'd love to go, Ryder."

He smiled and then he was quickly on top of me, lying between my legs. I became breathless and whispered, "What are you doing?"

He gave this boyish grin and said, "You weren't how I left you when I got back." He sat back on his knees and said, "Take the shirt off, Isabelle." I sat up, and without taking my eyes off him, I lifted the shirt up and over my head. The second I dropped the shirt on the floor, Ryder was ripping a condom open with his teeth.

He started to place the condom on his erection when I put my hand on top of his. I looked up into his eyes and said, "Can I do it?" Without blinking, Ryder nodded and I took the condom from him and he dropped his hands to his sides. I had the condom in my hand and it was like I had all the power. "Lie down, Ryder." He set his head on the pillow and lay there looking up at me with wonderment across his face. I straddled him and the second I rolled the condom on, I lifted my hips and lowered myself onto him.

I heard Ryder gasp and it felt like someone took over my body. I placed my hands on his chest and lifted my hips up and down over and over again. I straightened my back and my head was facing the ceiling. He was in so deep this way and it felt different from when he was on top. I felt his fingers grazing my arms and I looked down and we interlaced our fingers together.

By doing that I was able to get more leverage and moved up and down faster. My leg muscles began to burn but I didn't care. I felt the tension building and soon my orgasm was rolling through my body. Ryder sat up and sucked a nipple into his mouth. He wrapped his arms around my waist and my fingers were running through his hair.

Expertly I moved up and down his cock. While he was still sucking my nipple, one of his hands moved up into my hair and the other was grabbing my ass. The second Ryder moved to my other nipple I screamed his name and I felt his cock twitch inside me.

I was still shaky but managed to wrap my legs around his waist. We held on to each other for a while trying to catch our breath and then I started laughing. Ryder pulled away from me and looked at me curiously and I just started laughing more.

Ryder started to laugh along with me but through his laughter he asked, "What's so funny?"

I tried to control my laughter but I couldn't do it. After laughing a few more seconds, I said, "Is it like this for everyone? Because if it is, I don't understand how people can leave their houses."

Ryder started laughing while shaking his head back and forth. "Oh boy, I've created a monster—" He kissed me. "—but to answer your question, I'm not sure if it's like this for everyone. I can tell you right now I've never experienced anything like this before in my life. You know you've ruined me, Isabelle, right? There's no one else for me but you." He shrugged his shoulders and then wrapped my face in his hands and said, "For me, you're it."

Chapter 18

"Sweetheart, are you almost ready?"

I turned around and saw Ryder standing in my doorway with his luggage in his hands. "Almost, I just have to get my toiletries."

He smiled. "All right, I'll just be in the kitchen." I nodded, walked out of my room, and grabbed my shampoo, conditioner, and body wash. Packing everything away, I zipped my bag closed and carried it into the kitchen. Ryder was standing at the counter sipping his coffee with a huge grin on his face.

I walked over and placed my bag on the floor. "What are you smiling about?"

Ryder looked up into my eyes and said, "I'm just really excited."

I smiled at him and said, "I know the feeling."

Once Ryder finished his coffee we locked up our apartment and headed down to his car. After we finished loading our bags we were on our way to the airport for our flight to Las Vegas, Nevada for the tattoo convention. When we arrived at the airport, Ryder carried both of our bags in and we went through all of the different types of security checks that were required and then waited at the gate for our flight to be called.

Our flight was scheduled for 12:15 in the afternoon, and a half hour before I could tell there was a change in Ryder's mood. His knee started to bob up and down and I noticed that he'd started biting his lip. I was busy sipping my Starbuck's and looking at a magazine but I noticed his movements out of the corner of my eye. Closing my magazine, I placed it in my lap. "All right, what's the matter?"

He was in the middle of biting his nail but stopped and said, "I'm sorry." When he stopped biting his nails, his teeth started chattering. I put the magazine on the seat next to me, turned to him, and brought my legs up in the chair. "Ryder?"

He stopped grinding his teeth together and threw both of his hands up in the air. "I'm scared of flying."

I couldn't believe that this huge, muscular man was scared of flying. I couldn't help but let a little laugh escape and Ryder half glared, half smirked at me. "You aren't supposed to laugh at me. You're supposed to help me through this. That's what a girlfriend is supposed to do."

I completely let my laugh go. People around us were giving us weird stares but it didn't matter to me. We were never going to see them again. "Oh, munchkin. I'm not a normal girlfriend, am I? How about you just go over to the bar and have a drink? Maybe that'll calm your nerves."

He tilted his head to the side and made a noise. I knew he was thinking about it and within a matter of minutes he grabbed his wallet and walked off in the direction of the bar. Once I saw him sit down and put the beer to his lips, I picked up my magazine and went back to reading.

After a few drinks Ryder "walked" back over to me and plopped down in his chair. He had a huge smile plastered on his face and his blurry eyes were on me. I finished taking my last sip of coffee and smiled into my cup. After swallowing, I turned to him and said, "Are you feeling any better, stud?" Ryder just nodded his head and then pulled me into his lap for a kiss. I tried to push away from him because I knew people were staring at us but he was just so damn sexy that I got lost in his kiss.

Pulling away from him, I asked, "What was all that about?"

Ryder just shrugged his shoulders. "I'm just really excited is all." Once it was time for our plane to board we grabbed our bags and waited in line to board the plane. After getting all comfy in our seats, Ryder wrapped my hand in his and kissed it.

I inched over to him, kissed him on the cheek, told him to go to sleep, and that we would be there shortly. I knew he was still nervous but the alcohol was taking its toll on him. After wrapping him up in the blanket, I kissed him on the lips. I began to pull out the magazine from earlier when Ryder dropped the Kindle in my lap.

I looked over at him and he had this sheepish grin on his face. I picked up the Kindle and remembered it was the one he had gotten for me for

Christmas and then all of those bad memories came rushing back. I held it up and turned back to Ryder and said, "What's this for?"

I could tell he was nervous because he started to bite his lip but he whispered, "I just couldn't get rid of them." I started to tear up because I couldn't believe where we were just a few months ago and where we were now. I stood up from my seat and placed the Kindle in it and then slid over onto Ryder's lap and hugged him. He wrapped his arms around me and pulled me closer and I nuzzled into his neck, breathing in his scent.

I swear if I could bottle his scent and sell it, I would. There's just something about Ryder which made me feel so comfortable and relaxed. I could tell I did the same for him as well because I could feel his breath on me and he was playing with my hair and twirling it in his fingers. I kissed him on the neck and then whispered, "I'm so sorry."

He pulled away from me to look into my eyes and started to tear up. "I'm not, because I feel like we're right where we should be." He cupped my head in his hands and used the pads of his thumbs to wipe away my tears. "Please don't cry, Isabelle."

I sucked in a few breaths, wiped my tears away, and then smiled. Smiled because I couldn't believe just how lucky I was to be here with Ryder. Never in my life did I actually expect for things to turn around when I left for school in August, but here I am in April. For the first time in a really long time I'm happy and content with who I am.

After kissing him I got back in my seat and started up my Kindle. I knew the flight was going to be long, so I picked a book called *Blindfolded Innocence* and started to read, but not before wrapping my hand in Ryder's and saying, "I love you."

***

Ryder slept the entire flight while I read my book, which relieved me. After getting off the plane and collecting our luggage, we got a taxi and were on our way to the MGM Grand hotel. The ride over was completely silent. We were both in awe of our new surroundings and couldn't wait to have some fun. The convention was going to be tomorrow, April 14th, and then my 21st birthday was on April 15th, so we decided a celebration was in order.

After checking in, we were taken up to our room. I couldn't believe how gorgeous the room was. There was a king-size bed in the center with a plasma screen television on the opposite end of the wall. A little sitting area was in the corner, which consisted of a sofa with two end chairs and a coffee table. The bathroom was incredible with a Jacuzzi tub and a gorgeous shower with water heads coming from all different directions. But the view from our room was amazing. The windows stretched from floor to ceiling and you could see all of Vegas. The lights and buildings made me think of all sorts of trouble we could get ourselves in.

I was too busy taking in the scenery to notice Ryder walk into the bathroom and turn the water on for the Jacuzzi. I turned around and saw he was standing there in a plush robe and nothing else. He walked over to me and grabbed my hand. "Take a bath with me?" I just nodded and he walked backwards into the bathroom. He picked me up and plopped me on the counter then turned to check on the water temperature and filled the entire tub with bubbles.

Turning around, Ryder walked over to me and dropped his robe to the floor. "Lift your arms, Isabelle." I did so and he pulled my shirt over my head and undid my bra. The way he looked at me completely turned me on. Each time he saw me naked it was like he was finding something new about me. He stepped in between my legs and looked down at me. "I love you, Isabelle."

I wrapped my arms around his neck and said, "I love you, Ryder." He lifted me down from the counter and unbuckled my jeans and pulled them down along with my panties.

I thought we were going to get in the tub but Ryder lifted me back up onto the counter and said, "Open wide." I moved so my back was to the mirror and opened my legs for him. He pulled my bottom closer so I was hanging off the edge of the sink. Ryder bent down in front of me and lifted my legs so each one was on lying on his shoulders. After kissing my belly button and giving a soft pinch to both nipples, he stuck a finger inside me. I heard him gasp. "God, you're so wet." I just moaned in appreciation and he stuck in another finger.

At first I wanted to close my eyes but I was more intrigued to see what Ryder was doing. As soon as I looked down, I saw him watching me and then he started lapping me up. He spread my lips apart and licked me endlessly. We kept our eyes on one another the entire time and within seconds I was moaning and sucking his fingers deeper inside of me.

I was trying to catch my breath but I heard a condom wrapper being ripped open and then I felt him push inside me. I wrapped my arms and legs around him and kissed him forcefully. There was just something different about this time and I knew that we both felt it. While Ryder was thrusting into me, I kissed him on the lips. I started to pull away but he crushed his mouth to mine and deepened the kiss.

I felt water on my face and pulled away to see Ryder tearing up. I didn't understand what was going on. I thought maybe I was hurting him but he cupped my face in his hands and said, "I love you, Isabelle Clark."

I knew he loved me but the way he said it this time was different and by different I mean in a good way. With misty eyes and a quivering chin, I whispered, "I love you, Ryder." The second I said his name, he pushed into me one last time and we finished together. We never took our eyes off one another. Pulling out of me, he disposed of the condom, picked me up, wrapped me in his arms, and got in the tub. My back was to his front as he wrapped his arms around me and nuzzled his face in my neck. He pushed my hair to the other side and lightly kissed me. I placed my hands on top of his against my stomach and relaxed into him.

We just stayed like that for a while, cuddling up to one another, feeling totally and completely content. After washing one another, Ryder got out of the tub and then lifted me out and dried me off. He wrapped me in my robe and then dried himself off, which I found completely sexy because he took care of me before himself. We both got on the bed and Ryder wrapped his arms around me.

I intertwined my fingers in his and turned my head to look up at him. "What do you want to do tonight?"

He smiled. "This."

I smiled and said, "That sounds perfect," which earned me a kiss. Pulling away Ryder grabbed the hotel phone and ordered us some room service. We got a fresh fruit platter, sparkling wine, chocolate covered strawberries, and a cheese plate.

Everything was delicious but what made it better was that we fed one another. I always thought doing something like that would be annoying. I mean, I can feed myself but there was something sensual about it. We giggled and enjoyed every second and every bite of it.

Once the cart was taken away we got out of our robes and jumped under the covers and faced one another. Ryder was lightly grazing his fingers up and down my arm, giving me goose bumps. I wrapped my arms around him and squished my body up against his. I kissed him on the nose and heard Ryder whisper, "I love you so much, Isabelle."

I pulled away from and smiled. "Show me," and that's exactly what he did for the rest of the night and into the morning.

I started to squirm around because I was dreaming about Ryder doing things to me. I heard myself moan and my eyes popped open when I realized that my dream wasn't just a dream but that Ryder was actually doing it to me. He was sucking on one of my nipples and his finger was moving in and out of me. Through a yawn I said, "Mmm, I could get used to this."

He moved his lips up my body and kissed my neck and then kissed my lower lip. "Good, sweetheart," then he pushed inside and took me to the end.

Once we managed to get out of bed, we got ready and were on our way to the convention. Ryder was acting like a little kid, which was so adorable. The entire cab ride there Ryder's leg was bouncing up and down and he couldn't sit still. It was kind of humorous seeing this huge, muscled, tattooed man acting like a little kid. He was squealing and kept asking, "Are we there yet?" I was excited for the convention but I was more excited because I wanted Ryder to have a good time.

The cab didn't even come to a full stop before Ryder jumped out of the car and headed inside. After I paid the cabdriver, I ran up to meet Ryder, and after getting through we took in our surroundings. I couldn't believe how crazy it was. There were vendors, people tattooing, seminars, and clothing for sale.

I looked at Ryder—he seemed right in his element. We walked around for a while just looking at everything and Ryder was showing me all types of things. I knew tattooing was a passion of his but the way he talked today showed me just how much he truly loved it. He was so passionate and every word he said was filled with so much love. I loved Ryder, but watching him that day, I think I fell in love with him even more if that was possible.

I knew I looked stupid because of the huge smile on my face and I knew my eyes were twinkling. Ryder was in the middle of showing me all of these tattoo artists and their work when he turned to me and said, "What, sweetheart?"

I just shrugged my shoulders and said, "I hope I'm passionate about something one day the way you are about tattooing."

I couldn't help but giggle because he started to blush, but then he pulled me up against him and said, "I love tattooing, but it comes nowhere near in comparison to how much I love you, Isabelle Clark."

We stayed at the convention for a few hours and I got Ryder a shirt that read, *Sticks & Stones May Break My Bones But Whips, Chains, Tattoos & Piercings EXCITE ME!* We decided to head back to the hotel and get a nap in before my birthday dinner. I wasn't going to be able to drink tonight because Ryder said he had huge plans for me tomorrow.

Ryder had made reservations for 8 p.m. so I began to get ready at 6:30. I took a shower and shaved and washed everything twice. I applied mascara and a little bit of glitter eye shadow. After drying my hair, I did some lazy curls. I had packed a few dresses because I knew we would be going out to dinner for my birthday. I ended up choosing a peach colored dress which covered up everything in the front and went to my mid-thigh but the back was completely open. I ended up having to go braless because I didn't want the straps to show from the back and paired my dress with some gold heels. I added a few bangles and some perfume before I entered the bedroom, where Ryder was waiting for me.

His back was to me as he looked out at the view but at the sounds of my heels on the floor he turned around. He looked just as breathless as I felt. Ryder was wearing a grey suit with a black button up shirt. He'd left a few buttons unbuttoned at the top and my mouth started to water. His mouth fell open as I stood there with a huge smile on my face. That was exactly the reaction I had been going for. He started to open his mouth to tell me something but I put my finger up to stop him and slowly twirled around. He sucked in a huge breath. When my eyes met his again he looked hungry, and not just for food.

Within a few strides his hands were on my hips and his lips on mine. I wrapped my arms around him to try to deepen the kiss but he immediately stepped away. I tilted my head and scrunched my eyebrows together because I didn't understand.

Ryder started to laugh. "Sweetheart, if I don't stop now we won't leave this room the rest of the night."

Oh, I like that.

Ryder took me to dinner at *Fiamma Trattoria* and the food was amazing. I had the Grilled Salmon and Ryder had the New York steak. We had pleasant conversation throughout the entire dinner but I could tell Ryder was nervous. When he didn't think I was watching him I saw him bite his lip or scrunch his eyebrows together. Before the waiter came back with our receipt, Ryder pulled a black box out of his jacket pocket and set it down in front of me.

It was a long rectangular box so I knew it was going to be some sort of jewelry. I looked into Ryder's eyes and he put a finger to my lips. "I wanted to get you something and I don't want to hear you say anything about it. Okay?" I just nodded my head with his finger still to my lips and then kissed it. Once he pulled away I looked down at the box and slowly opened it. My mouth fell open. Inside was a necklace with a single diamond.

My heart was beating wildly. I couldn't believe how beautiful it was. I closed my eyes and the second I opened them a tear fell down. Ryder's hand was instantly to my face wiping away my tears. I looked up at him and he said, "Happy tears?" I just smiled and nodded.

I got out of my seat and sat in his lap and kissed him. It didn't matter to me that we were in a fancy restaurant and people were probably staring at us. When I pulled away, Ryder rested his forehead against mine and whispered, "I want you to wear that tonight." I started to take the necklace out of the box when Ryder put his hand on top of mine and looked me in the eyes. "Only that."

Once the door closed behind us, Ryder's hands were on my hips and his lips were on my neck. His front was to my back and I could feel how badly he wanted me. Ryder slowly untied the top of my dress and let it fall to the floor. He moved my hair to one side. I heard him open the box and then he placed the necklace around my neck. I picked the diamond up in my hand and looked at it. I couldn't believe how beautiful his gift was.

The second I let go of the necklace Ryder turned me around and I was standing there in my thong and the necklace. He walked me backwards until I felt the edge of the bed at the backs of my knees. Ryder leaned down in front of me and slowly took off my thong and then laid me down on the bed. He told me to scoot up to the end and I laid my head on the pillow.

He was standing at the edge, still in his suit. Without taking his eyes off me he took off his jacket, unbuttoned his shirt, and unbuckled his pants. He looked so beautiful—I bit my lower lip. He crawled up between my legs and started to suck and lick my nipples. I moaned but I didn't want foreplay. I just wanted him.

He moved up and kissed my lips and I put my hands in his hair. He leaned away from me and looked in my eyes. "I love you, Isabelle."

"I love you, Ryder." He started to move down my body but I kept my hands firmly in his hair. He looked at me because he didn't understand what was going on but I said, "I just want you."

The second his lips touched mine he slid right inside of me. We both moaned at the same time and then Ryder started to move. It was slow and deliberate. We were slowly building up to our orgasms. I started to feel my orgasm taking over my body when Ryder pulled out of me.

"Shit!" I got up on my elbows and looked at him. "I forgot to put on a condom. No wonder it felt so fucking good." He started to get off the bed but I pulled him back on top of me and wrapped my legs around him.

"Please, Ryder." He looked at me and I quickly said, "I'm on birth control. I just want to feel all of you." He kissed me again on the lips and slipped right back in.

He was kissing my neck and I was running my fingers up and down his back when I felt his movements become uneven. He tried to pull out but I kept my legs around him and he said, "Isabelle?"

As I whispered, "I love you, Ryder," we both finished.

Ryder pulled me onto his chest and then looked over at the clock. "Happy birthday, sweetheart. I hope it's a good one."

I just murmured, "It already is."

Chapter 19

I woke up the next morning and Ryder had breakfast set out for the two of us. He had ordered a fruit tray with some coffee and mimosas—after all, I was twenty-one. I put on my robe and Ryder kissed me on the lips and held out my chair for me. After pushing me in, he sat in the seat across from mine and in his hand appeared a single pink rose. "For my sweetheart."

I took the rose from him and smiled. We ate and talked and afterwards Ryder told me to get ready. He told me that he had planned a full day at the spa for me to relax. I took a quick shower and put on a tank top with some yoga pants. I was in the middle of brushing my teeth when there was a knock on the door. Ryder yelled from the bed, "Sweetheart, could you get that?" With my toothbrush still in my mouth I turned the knob to our door and heard, "SURPRISE!"

Sarah, Gabe, Jade, Jason, Ashlynn, Derrick, and Patrick were all standing there with huge smiles on their faces and carrying balloons. My toothbrush fell from my mouth and I turned my head to see Ryder had this huge smile on his face and he said, "Surprise." I turned back to everyone and said, "Well come on in." After everybody gave us hugs and looked around the room and sat down I asked, "So what's going on?" Ryder walked over and wrapped me in his arms. "I thought since it's your birthday and Sarah and Gabe need Bachelor and Bachelorette parties, we could combine the two. Since it's your 21st birthday, we were just going to have one big party and celebrate everything."

I smiled and kissed him on the cheek. "That sounds awesome." For a few minutes we all hung out and then Ryder looked at his phone. "All right, Sarah, Jade, Ashlynn, Patrick, and Isabelle. You all have appointments at the spa, so get going. You're getting your nails and hair done along with massages and facials." Ryder kissed me on the lips. "Have a good time, sweetheart."

***

We were so excited to have a day to just get pampered and relax. Plus I couldn't wait to meet up with everyone later to go out clubbing for my 21st birthday. Arriving at the spa, we had to change into comfy robes and plush slippers and were given mimosas along with hot green tea and water.

We were taken to our own private room where we were given our manicures and pedicures at the same time and could enjoy one another's company. Patrick kept going on and on about how gorgeous

Ryder was and how he was so happy we were back together and everybody else nodded in agreement. I ended up choosing pink for my fingers and toes and then we were into another room for our facials and massages.

I had never had a facial before but it felt amazing. After the lady applied creams, she wrapped my face up in a hot towel and I swear I could have died in that moment a happy person. After she wiped my face clean and applied some jasmine oils, the lights were turned down and soft music began to play. I was lying face down on a cushioned table and the masseuse worked his magic. I felt so much tension taken away and I began to fall asleep on the table. He worked every kink I had out of my neck and relaxed my muscles. The massages were for thirty minutes but it felt like five. Once our massages were finished, we were taken into a room with a table filled with finger foods and drinks. We all sat around the table and there were cucumber sandwiches, sweet pastries, and fruit with yogurt.

We all felt so relaxed but then Patrick started a conversation. "So, Ashlynn. Chickadee, what do you plan on doing about Jason?"

I thought I knew the answer but she said, "I don't care. I'm over it and I'm moving on."

A part of me was sad because I knew they would be really cute together but the other part was happy for her because she had made a decision. We all gave her our approval but Jade said, "Dammit, that brother of mine is so fucking stupid! I swear if a piano fell on his head he wouldn't know the damn difference!" We sat around and gossiped for a little bit more but we were all tired from our massages so we decided to go back to our rooms to take naps before going out tonight.

***

I was napping when I felt arms around me. I snuggled up closer and murmured, "Hi."

Ryder kissed me on the cheek and said, "Hi, birthday girl. Have you been having fun so far today?"

I nodded my head. "What about you? What have you guys been up to?"

Ryder informed me that he, Gabe, Jason, and Derrick had gone down to the casino and did some gambling. I turned around in his arms and kissed him on the lips and snuggled into him. Ryder pulled the blanket over us and said, "Sleep, sweetheart, because we have a long night ahead of us."

I decided to curl my hair and put it in a side ponytail with some diamond earrings and the necklace Ryder gave me. My dress was a violet strapless number. It was tight at the top and showed off the girls then flowed around my hips and ended around mid-thigh. I paired the dress with some high black heels along with a black clutch.

We all met in the front of the hotel and decided on *Pearl* for dinner—it was delicious. For my first drink as a legal twenty-one year old was a Cotton Candy Martini, which was amazing. The presentation was actually pretty cool because the waiter brought the glass over topped with pink cotton candy and then poured the alcohol in. The drink was pretty sweet and strong, so I sipped it slowly but I loved that I could finally order a drink and give my actual ID. Once we paid for dinner we headed to *Chateau Nightclub & Gardens* to start off our long night.

Ryder had a table reserved for us so we didn't need to worry about finding a place to sit or having to wait long for our drinks. Ryder ordered champagne to celebrate my birthday and Sarah and Gabe's wedding. After everybody sang, "Happy Birthday" to me we were ready to party the night away!

***

I woke up and it felt like somebody had crawled into my brain and shook it. Every move I made felt like I was going to literally die and I was barely capable of moving my head to the side when I saw Ryder staring at me with this stupid ass smile on his face. "Good morning, sweetheart." I grumbled a hello to him and he laughed so hard that he shook the bed.

I tried to yell at him but even whispering was making me nauseous. Ryder must have been able to tell because he got off the bed and walked into the bathroom. He came back over to my side of the bed and handed me two aspirin and a bottle of water. My arm was covering up my face when he nudged me. I slightly opened one eye to peek up at him.

He leaned down and kissed me on the nose then said, "Take these and drink ALL of this." I managed to sit up and take the pills then downed the water within seconds. I noticed it was still dark outside and I looked over at him. "Why is it still dark out? What time is it?"

Ryder lay back down on the bed, dragged me over to him and said, "Early. So how about you get some more rest before we have to check out at noon?" As soon as he said I could sleep longer, I drifted off in his arms.

The second time I woke up I felt so much better. I had a slight headache but I was acting like a somewhat "normal" human being. I heard the shower was on so I slipped out of my panties and found Ryder in the shower naked and completely beautiful. I opened the shower door and walked in behind him. I wrapped my arms around him.

I heard him chuckle and then he asked, "How are you feeling?"

I rested my head in the center of his back and mumbled, "Better."

He turned around and looked down at me. "What do you remember from last night, Isabelle?"

The second he asked my heart stopped. I remembered dinner, the birthday song, and some of the dancing, but after that I didn't remember much of anything. I bit my lip because I could see fuzzy mental images but couldn't really form a clear picture.

Ryder put his thumb on my lip and said, "Let go, sweetheart." I let go of my lower lip and he kissed me. I wrapped my arms around him and he lifted me up and leaned my back against the shower wall.

He pulled his head away from me and said, "You're a cute drunk."

I accidentally slammed my head back against the shower wall but I didn't have time to think about it because Ryder kissed me. He pushed his tongue inside my mouth and then pulled back and said, "I love you."

After our little romp in the shower, we got ready and packed up our things. Ryder told me that everybody else had to get an earlier flight so they were already at the airport. I'd almost forgotten about him saying I was a cute drunk, because he was making me moan his name but now that I had a clear head I said, "So what did I do last night, exactly?"

I looked at him and he had this huge smile on his face while he zipped up his bag. I put my hand on my hip. "Ryder?"

He looked over at me and had this cocky grin on his face. "You might want to sit down for this." Before I sat down I grabbed a bottle of water and took a few sips. He sat down in front of me and started laughing.

He kept laughing and then I started laughing. "All right, Ryder, what exactly did I do?"

He tried to stop laughing but he said, "Well, you were dancing with Ashlynn, Jade, Sarah, and Patrick for a while. I was sitting on the couches with Gabe, Jason, and Derrick just bullshitting when this girl walked up and asked if I wanted to dance with her. I wanted to get a rise out of you so I walked out onto the dance floor with her. We weren't dancing provocatively or anything but you saw us and I swear your face turned bright red. I thought you were going to knife the girl or something but you danced your way in and well, we pretty much had sex on the dance floor."

He must have seen the stunned look on my face because he backtracked and said, "We didn't actually have sex, but um, people started watching us and after the song was over you yelled, 'This is my man. Back it up, bitches!' I started laughing and then you jumped into my arms and kissed me."

I couldn't believe that I'd actually done that but I felt like he was leaving something out.

Something that was very important.

"Oh god, what song was on exactly?" His face turned into this evil smirk. "Turnin' Me On."

I doubled over in laughter and tried to catch my breath. "Well, no wonder I did that because that's my song!" He picked me up in his lap and kept laughing. "What are you not telling me?"

He said, "You should probably see this." He handed me his phone and I pressed *Play*.

I saw Ryder sitting in a chair on stage and there was a girl facing him giving him a lap dance. I was getting ready to yell at him because some bitch gave him a lap dance when the girl turned around and, holy shitballs, it was me.

Damn, I look hot!

I was swaying my hips and grinding my ass into Ryder's crotch. Even on a video camera I could tell from the look in his eyes that he wanted me. That I was his everything. Just watching the video was making me wet and I sat down on Ryder's lap and felt his erection. Ryder wrapped his arm around me and started to push his hand in the waist of my yoga pants while his other hand was pinching and pulling my nipples through the tank top.

I moaned in appreciation but then Ryder pushed me off him and set me on the sofa while he started walking around the room. I was going to ask him what the matter was when he looked at me and said, "I have an idea."

"Okay?"

He walked up to me then started pacing back and forth, still looking at me. "What if we got married?" I thought he was joking around, so I started to laugh but he knelt in front of me and said, "Think about it. I mean we're in Vega—"

I stood up and started yelling. "Ryder Mitchell, what is the matter with you? Are you cra—?" I didn't get to finish saying *crazy* because he pushed me up against the wall and began to kiss me. I mean, really kiss me.

He swept his tongue along my lower lip and begged for entrance. I got so lost in the kiss that I forgot what we were yelling about and immediately wrapped my arms around him. Ryder lifted me up and I wrapped my legs around and pulled him closer. I wanted to feel him up against me. I wanted him to be inside me.

I moaned against his mouth and he sucked my lower lip and bit down but then he pulled away and cupped my face in his hands. "Isabelle Clark, I'm very serious about marrying you. Maybe not right now, because I can see that you're a little freaked out, but I plan on making you Mrs. Mitchell someday. I just want you to know that."

It always seemed like when he didn't want to hear what I had to say he was kissing me or pushing his fingers inside me like he was doing right now. He pushed his hand inside the waist of my yoga pants and then slipped two fingers inside while his thumb put pressure on my clit. He kissed my mouth but I shook my head.

He moved back a little to look at me. "Just fuck me, Ryder." I was still up against the wall and somehow Ryder was able to yank off my yoga pants while I unbuckled his jeans and pushed them down with my feet still wrapped around him. He sprung free from his boxers and he expertly ripped off my thong. Before I could say, "Please," he was slamming inside me.

At this angle I thought I was going to come any minute but then I noticed something was different and I started to quiver. Ryder was sucking my neck and biting down a bit hard when I grabbed the back of his head a little hard so he would look at me. I squinted my eyes at him and he smirked and said, "Oh, I put the piercing in. I mean, when in Vegas…" and pulled all of the way out and then slammed back into me.

I grabbed ahold of him and held on with all my might. He kept slamming into me and my back was hitting the wall but I didn't care how loud we were being or how many calls were probably being made to the front desk about loud noises. I blocked out the pictures falling from the wall and focused on Ryder. He was thrusting into me and all I concentrated on were our bodies slamming together and our grunts and moans.

He started to slow down and caress my nipple but I said, "I. Want. It. Hard."

He moved away to look into my face and said, "Are you sure?"

I bit my lip and said, "Yes."

A sly grin replaced the questioning look and he moved his head to bite my earlobe. He whispered in my ear, "Hold on tight, sweetheart."

I wrapped my arms around him and before I knew it he was pulling out and slamming into me. "Oh God, yes!"

"Oh, fuck, sweetheart," Ryder groaned while holding my hips steady and slamming into me.

I noticed he was looking down, watching our bodies meet, and I followed his line of sight. "Fuck, that's hot." Ryder had a stunned look when he looked back at me and then with his eyes on mine, he rubbed my clit harder than he ever had and before I knew it we were coming.

After we managed to catch our breaths, Ryder put me down on wobbly legs and kissed me on the lips. Picking up our luggage, we walked to our door, and as Ryder held the door open for me he said, "Let's go home."

***

The month after returning from Vegas was almost completely taken up with Maid of Honor duties. Somehow I also managed to complete my junior year of college despite spending so much time helping Sarah pick out her wedding dress. It took many shots of tequila, but Jade, Ashlynn, and I finally convinced her to choose one.

We had managed to get everything else done besides the dress. Of course you have to save the best for last, or maybe the worst; whichever way you see finding your wedding dress.

Cake. *Check!*

Flowers. *Check!*

Pastor. *Check!*

Wedding Dress. *Complete Disaster!*

We had been to countless bridal stores and Sarah had tried on numerous wedding dresses but she kept talking about some bullshit where when you try it on then you'll know. Whatever that meant!

I had told Sarah in the morning that she had to have a dress by the end of the day or Jade, Ashlynn, and I would pick, which surprisingly she was totally fine with. We had decided to go back to the first store we had visited in our journey of finding the "perfect" wedding dress. Sarah had tried on five dresses but still couldn't decide. She walked out of the fitting room and her head was slouched over and she was huffing and puffing. "This is hopeless."

As her Maid of Honor, I told the bitch to sit down and Jade, Ashlynn, and I would go on a scavenger hunt. I decided we would each pick out a dress for Sarah to try on and those were her options. I chose a beautiful mermaid inspired dress. It was tight until the hip and then flowed out in layers and had sparkles all over it. Ashlynn chose an enchanted, lace style wedding gown. It was form fitting and would have suited Sarah very well. Jade chose a dress with lots of glitz and glam. It was a ball gown with diamond glitter all over it.

Sarah was a sport and tried on all three dresses and she looked gorgeous in every single one. After she tried on the last dress she said, "All right, don't be mad."

Oh fucking shit! Bitch isn't picking any of them. Hold me back because I might knife her!

All three of us gave Sarah the fakest smiles ever and through gritted teeth I said, "What, Sarah?"

She started pulling at the dress and biting her lip. I could tell she was nervous because she had dragged Jade, Ashlynn, and I around and she still hadn't picked a dress. She took a deep breath and looked all of us in the eye before she said, "I've decided on a dress!"

At this point we couldn't have given a rat's ass which dress she chose because all that mattered was that the psycho had finally picked one, but of course Jade asked, "So which of the three options did you choose?"

Sarah began to laugh nervously. "None. I'm going to go change into the dress I chose." The second she went in the dressing room all three of us looked at each other because during this complete disaster she had chosen her dress and this could have ended forever ago but I became a little curious as to which one.

Still in the dressing room, Sarah yelled, "Close your eyes!" All three of us eye rolled and then covered our faces with our hands. I could hear Sarah walking out because her heels were clicking against the floor and the dress was gliding across the floor towards us. I heard her step on the landing and she said, "Okay, you girls can open your eyes."

The second my hand left my face, I heard Jade scream, "You have got to be fucking kidding me! That's the first goddamn dress!"

Sarah started to laugh and said, "Yeah, I know. Every other dress I tried on didn't make me feel that thing. I knew if I didn't pick this dress I would regret it later." She started biting her lip again and I just laughed because we all loved that dress and had wanted her to pick that one but she kept saying, "I just want to see what else is out there."

The second we got over the initial shock, all three of us smiled because Sarah looked beautiful in the dress. It was form-fitting then spread out at the knee. It was lace material that dipped in the front and the back was completely bare. The veil was lace as well and the dress had a little bit of everything.

Elegance.

Romance.

Chic and Modern.

Glamorous.

At the sight of us smiling, Sarah's eyes started to tear up and she yelled, "I'm getting married!" We all started jumping up and down and then Sarah looked between Jade, Ashlynn, and myself and said, "Who do you think will be next?"

Chapter 20

Summer had finally begun and school was no longer in session. Mrs. Bee offered me a full time summer job at the library but I declined. Ashlynn begged me to work with her but I've been working my ass off this entire year and I need a break.

A long one.

I think I deserve it.

I still worked with Patrick at the bookstore. If you consider "working" hanging out with your friend and bullshitting the entire day while reading, then yeah, I work.

I'd decided that my summer would consist of reading all the books I bought on my Kindle and writing my first novel. It's a play on my life with Ryder that I entitled, *Ours*. While we have gone through some crazy shit, I wouldn't change anything because it's ours and it all started with an idea.

I was halfway through reading a book when Ryder walked into the living room and plopped down on the couch with me. He lifted my legs and cradled them in his lap and began to massage my feet.

The second he walked into a room, nothing else mattered. All I see is him. I held the Kindle in front of my face to hide my huge smile when Ryder said, "I have an idea."

If it's possible, my smile widened and I said, "What?"

Ryder's hand encompassed my Kindle and he placed it on the coffee table, never taking his eyes off me. "I want to take you to the beach."

Even though I'd never been to the beach and hate the idea, I go along with it because being with Ryder is all that really matters to me. I began to stand up when Ryder grabbed me around my hips and I fell back into his lap.

He whispered in my ear, "Where do you think you're going?"

I tilted my head to look at him and said, "I have to pack bag and get myself ready for our day at the beach."

He's kissing the back of my neck when he murmured, "Bags are ready. You just have to get yourself into some sexy-ass bikini." I pulled myself up from the couch and this time Ryder allowed me but not before playfully slapping me on the ass.

I walked back to my bedroom, even though I haven't slept in there for a while, it's still mine.

It's my sanctuary.

It's where I'm writing my first novel.

I walked over to my closet and picked out the only bikini I have. The top is strapless and pink while the bottoms are a baby blue with ties on either end. I changed into my bikini, put my jean shorts and tank top back on, and put on some flip-flops. I started to walk out of my room but I stop in my tracks. With my hand still on the knob, I looked around and all of the memories from this year came crashing back to me like a tidal wave.

Moving in.

Going to meet Ryder's parents.

Our first kiss.

Our first fight.

Our first ... everything.

I'm still smiling and looking around when Ryder's hands wrapped around my waist and he kissed my neck. "Ready, sweetheart?"

I closed my eyes and smiled. "Yeah, I think I am."

For the first time in my life I wasn't questioning anything.

I'm just going with it.

I'm being selfish and thinking about myself for once and what I want is everything that I've been given this year.

Friendship.

Love.

A future.

Getting everything in the car, we began our car ride to the beach. It's a comfortable silence and Ryder's holding my hand. The music's off and all I hear is the wind blowing past me because my other hand is hanging outside the car and I'm brought back to the car ride up to school when I was thinking about how my life was going to change.

I had an idea that my life would be different, but I never realized how drastically. If you would have told me back in August where I would be right now, I would have laughed in your face and said, "Quit bullshitting me." But now I realize that anything is possible and that I am special.

I have my sunglasses on and I looked out at the scenery around me and started to tear up. I thought about my life with Cynthia and how she was wrong.

How I am important.

How I am beautiful.

I lift my hand and begin to wipe the stray tears away and Ryder looks over. "You okay, Isabelle?"

I lift my sunglasses and look over at Ryder while smiling. "I am now."

Ryder found a parking spot, then carried our bags to the beach. It's sunny out but there aren't a lot of people around. I'm totally okay with that. We laid down our blankets and stripped off our clothing. After applying suntan lotion, I stretched out on my towel but Ryder had other ideas for us. He lifted me up over his shoulders and runs into the ocean. The water splashed all over us and I laughed, having the time of my life. He placed me down in the water and I wrapped my arms around him and kissed him.

We spent the rest of the day lounging on our towels, playing in the water, and building sandcastles.

The sun was beginning to set and Ryder sat behind me. I'm leaned up against him. His head is on my shoulder and we watched the sunset. He played with my fingers and then said, "So did I change your mind about the beach?"

I giggled. "I still hate it but I'd come here anytime with you."

He smiled. "Maybe this will change your mind." I looked down and Ryder had a little black box in his hand. My heart stopped and tears welled up in my eyes. I tried my damnedest not to let them fall but I closed my eyes to try and catch my breath, and the second my eyes close the tears fall.

Ryder heard me sniffling and came around in front of me. He kneeled down, looking into my eyes and said, "Sweetheart?"

I started to laugh and cry. For the first time in my life I'm speechless. I looked into his eyes. I see he's tearing up, too. Taking my left hand, he said, "Isabelle, you're the only thing in this life that makes sense. Without you, I have nothing. No ideas. No dreams. No possibilities."

I placed both my hands on my face because I didn't know what to say, and then he looked down and opened the box. There's a ring. He picked the ring up in his fingers and held it up.

Choking through his words, Ryder said, "The ring is simple with a diamond and a plain gold band, but it symbolizes our time together. We have been on a roller coaster ride this entire year and I think we deserve some simplicity. That's what this ring is, because asking you to marry me is the simplest thing ever.

"I had an idea forever ago for you to move in with me, and it's the best thing that has ever happened to me. I thought I knew all there was to know about life and then you ran into mine. The second I saw you I knew one day you were going to be Mrs. Mitchell. Before I had time to think or breathe, all of the pieces were falling together and now we're here. And as simple as taking my next breath I can say that I want you forever. So, Isabelle Katherine Clark … Will you marry me?"

The only thing I could do was smile and cry because I couldn't believe where my life was. And I could only imagine where it's going to go. I started thinking about it and what I'm certain of is that Ryder is in it. I looked into his eyes for just a couple of seconds, probably the longest of his life, and then I smile. I placed my hands on his cheeks and with so much certainty I whispered, "Yes."

Chapter 21

Ryder

It's been two years since I ran into this beautiful girl who would change my entire life. I still can't believe that she took a chance on a guy like me. She literally saved me from myself. We've been through a lot.

Some good.

Some bad.

Some incredibly amazing.

Some horribly awful.

But I wouldn't change a damn thing, because here we are today.

"Gabe. Are you positive that she hasn't changed her mind? You sure she hasn't run off with the pool boy or some shit like that? I mean really, you are 110% she'll walk out those doors over there?" I pointed over at the hotel where we were all staying.

Gabe smiled and patted me on the back. "Ryd, calm down, okay? That girl loves you, so don't worry about anything. Weddings never go exactly as planned. I mean, come on? You remember mine, don't you?" I smiled at the memory.

Sarah and Gabe got married the summer after junior year in Sarah's backyard. Their wedding was just immediate friends and family and was really beautiful. I walked Sarah down the aisle since her dad died from cancer when she was younger. Sarah thought it would be a cute idea for Rufus to be the ring bearer, but that idea turned into a complete and utter disaster when the Pastor asked for the rings and I saw that Rufus had eaten Gabe's ring. I thought Sarah was going to cry, but she just started laughing and looked up at the sky. "Oh no, you don't! I'm marrying this sexy, gorgeous man whether you like it or not! Ring or not, he's mine!" A couple days after the wedding I finally got the ring back for Gabe and Sarah.

I knew without a doubt in my mind that Gabe would be my best man and Isabelle chose Patrick to be her "man of honor." We decided to keep our wedding intimate so just our small group of friends and my family were there. It seemed like everything worked out just the way it was supposed to.

I tried to convince Isabelle to call her mom, but she never did. I didn't really push her too much on the matter because I couldn't believe that somebody would beat down my beautiful sweetheart. It broke my heart that her own mother didn't see the beautiful girl everybody else got to know. The girl I fell in love with that I was marrying today.

After I proposed to Isabelle on the beach, her mind was set that she wanted to get married on the beach. She thought it would be a cool idea that we get married at sunset because I proposed at sunset. She used to hate the beach even though she had never been there, but I changed her mind on that one after the proposal.

The icing on the cake was that after she whispered, "Yes," we made love on the beach and again in the ocean. I smiled just at the thought and all of the memories we had made and how many more we were going to create together.

But back to reality, I literally started to freak the fuck out. I felt like I was sweating bullets. I was wearing a pair of tan khaki pants and a white button down shirt with a few buttons unbuttoned at the top. I was barefoot. We wanted to keep our wedding casual and fun. The only thing that really mattered to Isabelle and me was that in the end we would be married.

You get married because you're in love. That's what matters the most. That's what's important, not all the hoopla and crazy stuff. I told Isabelle that I would be glad just getting married at the courthouse because I couldn't wait to marry the girl and finally make her mine. But she told me that our friends and my family had to be there. So while we were going through our senior year of college we were also planning a wedding. Jokingly, I would complain all the time, but Isabelle's only response were words that I had used on her earlier in our relationship. *Patience is a virtue.*

Goddamn, what is taking so long? It feels like an hour has gone by. What if she changed her mind? What if she realized there was somebody else out there that was ten times, ten million times better for her than me?

I started psyching myself out but then the music started and everybody stood up. My heart literally skipped a beat I was so nervous. And then I looked up and the view took my breath away. In that instant everything changed. Isabelle was standing at the end of the beach looking like an angel. A beautiful angel. My angel.

Her hair had grown a few inches and it was in waves running down her back. Her dress was strapless, flowing in the wind and she was barefoot. I couldn't wait to get my sweetheart barefoot and pregnant. She was carrying a bouquet of Ambrosia, and when I looked into her eyes, she smiled and winked at me.

Damn, what I wouldn't do for that girl. My girl. I really would do anything. There are people who say things, but they don't actually mean them. Actions are what really matter. Words are amazing, but actions … they're beautiful.

My heart is beating out of my chest and she's only a quarter of the way down the makeshift aisle, which was scattered with white rose petals. It looked like she was walking a bit faster than normal. I was starting to wonder if she had a change of heart, but then she broke out in a run toward me, to me. I couldn't take it anymore and ran to meet her halfway. When I finally reached her, I picked her up and spun her around, but before I could put her back in the sand I kissed her on those beautiful lips of hers. She dropped the bouquet in the sand, wrapped her arms around my neck, and began to play with the ends of my hair. I was so caught up in Isabelle's kiss that I almost missed the laughter and cheers coming from all around us.

After setting her down, we both looked around and started to laugh. I finally looked back at Isabelle and there was a blush on her beautiful face. "You ready, sweetheart?"

She started to giggle. "More than you know."

I took her hand in mine and we gladly walked back up to the preacher together. Out of the corner of my eye I saw Gabe smiling and then I looked across from him and saw tears coming down Sarah's face. She was always a hopeless romantic. Still is.

After I kissed my sweetheart on the cheek and winked at her, I looked toward the preacher and nodded for him to begin.

The preacher looked between us and then looked out at our family and friends. "Well, that was some introduction, everybody!"

All I could hear was cheering and laughter but it played in the background because I was so focused on the beautiful girl staring back at me.

"You know I have done a lot of weddings in my lifetime, but it is a rare treasure to see two people who are so completely in love with one another and I am deeply honored to bring those two together in marriage today. Now I heard that you both have written your own vows. So Ryder, how about you get started on that. Whenever you're ready."

The preacher handed me the microphone and I could feel my hands shaking. I had written a beautiful love letter to Isabelle. I always liked to be prepared, but the words I wrote didn't even come close to how I felt about this amazing girl. After looking at her, I realized that it just had to come from the heart, in the moment.

When I looked down into her big brown beautiful eyes, I couldn't help but tear up. I don't think for the life of me I'll ever get over Isabelle choosing me. Wanting me. So, I took a few breaths and shrugged my shoulders to try and calm myself, but it was no use.

"Isabelle. My sweetheart. I thought I knew all there was to know about love. Life. And then I met you. Well, I ran into you and all of that changed. You showed me how things could be. Should be. I thank God every day for the day you ran into my life and I will be in His debt for as long as I live. There are no words to describe how you make me feel. But I have an idea; that for as long as I live, I will show you just how much you mean to me. I love you. Forever and always."

I was choking up and saw tears rolling down my beautiful girl's face. It was just instinct that I put my hand on her cheek and wiped them away. I looked into her eyes and mouthed the words *I love you, Isabelle*.

Another tear rolled down her face and she mouthed back *I love you, Ryder*.

At that moment the preacher said, "All right, Isabelle, it's your turn. Whenever you're ready."

I handed her the microphone and I could see her hand shaking. She was struggling and I just had to touch her, to comfort her. I grabbed her left hand in mine and held onto it. She looked down at our intertwined fingers, smiled, and then looked up into my eyes. She took a few more deep breaths and then spoke the most beautiful words I had ever heard.

"Ryder. I have grown up my entire life being put down. Hearing that I'm not good enough and that I'm nothing. After twenty years of hearing those words, you start to believe them. That all changed the day I met you. I never thought I would be the lucky girl who you would fall in love with. I never even believed that this type of love would happen for me. Or that it even existed. The bonus is that it's with you.

"You have shown me that I am worth it, that it's okay to just be me. And for that I can't thank you enough. You have opened my heart and my mind to new possibilities and I will spend the rest of my life being eternally grateful to you. It has taken us a while to get where we are today, but I wouldn't change anything because it's our story; our beautiful story. And it all started with an idea; a beautiful idea. I love you, Ryder Mitchell."

I thought I was done crying but after hearing those beautiful words, I bawled. I couldn't believe that I did that for the beautiful girl standing in front of me. I could hear people wiping their eyes and blowing their noses in the audience, but I still couldn't manage to break away from looking at her. We both smiled at one another and looked up at the preacher, waiting for him to continue. We both started laughing when we saw the preacher was tearing up.

He wiped his eyes and then looked at me. "All right then. Ryder Tyler Mitchell. Do you take Isabelle Katherine Clark to be your forever? To love her. Cherish her. For the rest of your life?"

"I do."

"Isabelle Katherine Clark. Do you take Ryder Tyler Mitchell to be your forever? To love him. Cherish him. For the rest of your life?"

"I do."

Before she could even finish saying, "I do," I grabbed her head and smashed her lips to mine. She moaned into my mouth and wrapped her arms around my neck like I was her lifeline and she was never going to let go. I slowly moved my hands down to her hips and wrapped my arms around her and lifted her off the ground.

The preacher just laughed and said, "Uh, well, I guess Mr. and Mrs. Ryder Mitchell can just keep kissing. Congratulations."

There was hollering and whistling all around us but I was way too caught up in the kiss. I was starting to get lost in it and I knew if I didn't let her go in the next couple of seconds then there was no way we would make it to the reception. As much as I didn't want to, I kissed her one last time and set her back down on the sand.

"Really? But we were just getting started. I'm cool as a cucumber not going to the reception and just starting the honeymoon early."

Ugh, what I wouldn't give to start the honeymoon right now. "Did you really just say cool as a cucumber?"

She laughed and poked me in the chest. "Hey now, don't judge me. You knew my flaws before you married me. You're stuck with me for the rest of your life, Ryder Mitchell."

I smiled and kissed her again on the lips. "Yes, I am, Mrs. Mitchell, and damn proud of it."

She had this huge grin on her face.

"What's with the huge smile, wife?"

She shook her head and said, "That has a nice ring to it. I like you saying Mrs. Mitchell."

I smiled back at her. "Well, I love saying Mrs. Mitchell."

***

The reception was amazing, the food was delicious, and the dancing was so much fun. I couldn't believe this was our wedding. We had set up a bunch of cabanas with dance floors on the beach. It was a very romantic atmosphere with twinkle lights and sparklers. We chose a bunch of bite size appetizers for the food. I finally managed to get Isabelle to eat sushi and she loved it. Of course she still wouldn't go anywhere near the raw fish so she ate the avocado rolls. But hey, I won't complain.

One of the best parts were the speeches. Gabe's speech was thoughtful and endearing. He talked about how he was so glad his best friend found the love of his life and how he couldn't wait to see the next chapter in our lives together and what our future together holds. Sarah, on the other hand, just said, "Well, it's about damn time! Cheers, everybody!"

The best part of the night was our first dance. Throughout our entire relationship we never really had a song to call our own. Although Isabelle thought it would be funny if we danced to *Turnin' Me On* by Lil Wayne and Keri Hilson. I told her that would be our first dance in the bedroom. She winked at me and said, "Oh definitely!"

Seriously though, can the honeymoon start already? She's already turning me on.

Like the tattoo, Isabelle told me I had free rein. She said no song could ever get across how she felt about me. Of course there was no song that could perfectly describe how I felt about her but this one came close.

We were all sitting around talking with one another and joking when the lights went down. I wanted it to be a surprise so I told the DJ to turn the lights down when he was ready for our first dance. I was shaking because I was so damn nervous, but I bent down next to my wife and said, "Dance with me." She happily put her hand in mine and I led her on to the dance floor.

As soon as the chords started over the loud speakers Isabelle took a sharp intake of breath and looked up into my eyes. I could see tears welling up so I used my thumb to wipe them away. "Please don't cry, sweetheart. You have no idea what that does to me."

She sniffled a bit and then said, "I just … I never thought I would so lucky. This song is perfect." The song I'd chosen was *Then* by Brad Paisley.

I wiped the few remaining tears that fell from my beautiful wife's face and pulled her up close to me. The lyrics explained how I felt in a way that I couldn't. She was my reason for breathing. My air.

I just couldn't help but sing every word to her. Thinking about where we were. Where we are. Where we're going.

I heard sniffling and leaned down to look into my beautiful wife's face. I put her head in my hands and used my thumbs to wipe away the tears that fell. "Sweetheart, what's wrong?"

She pulled me even closer and kissed me on the chest. "That was just beautiful, Ryder. Your voice was what made the dance perfect. Is that really how you felt about me?"

I looked at her like she was crazy. "Sweetheart, if I could've married you the day I met you, you bet your sweet little ass I would have. I just can't believe that this is where my life has brought me and I can't thank you enough." I wrapped my arms around Isabelle and picked her up. She wrapped her arms around my neck and kissed me like her life depended on it.

I know mine did.

Once the song ended I was so ready to get the hell out of there. I didn't want to but I put her down and kept her hand in mine while I dragged her back to the table. I heard giggling from behind me, but I was a man on a mission. I just wanted to give a quick thanks to everybody and to tell everybody to enjoy their night when I heard a loud crash and my heart dropped. I turned around because I thought maybe my sweetheart might have run into something, but I saw Sarah hunched over and Gabe's face was as white as a ghost. Isabelle and I ran over and saw that there was a pool of water underneath Sarah. I looked at Isabelle and knew what the right thing to do was, but then someone interrupted our mind conversation.

"Oh no, you don't! Don't even think about skipping your honeymoon because this watermelon has decided to come a week early. Gabe and I will be fine, so you two get a move on and enjoy your honeymoon."

I let go of Isabelle and gave Sarah a hug and kissed her on the forehead. I then turned to Gabe and gave him a pat on the back and shook his hand. "You ready, Dad?"

His face just lit up and he said, "You can say that again."

After Isabelle gave her hugs to Sarah and Gabe, I grabbed her hand and dragged her out of the cabana. We were halfway to the car but then I felt a pull against my arm and saw that Isabelle was stopping where she stood and was bending over.

"Uh, sweetheart. What are you doing?"

She started to pull up her dress and said, "My shoes are killing me. Just let me take them off, okay?"

My eyes bugged out of my head. "Don't even think about it, sweetheart. If it's up to me, those will be staying on your feet the entire night."

She blushed and I swooped her up into my arms before she could react to my comment. "In a rush, Mr. Mitchell?"

I looked down at her in my arms. "You bet I am, Mrs. Mitchell."

She started to blush again and I wondered if it would ever get old seeing my wife blush at the things I said. After closing the door behind us in the limo, we were finally all set to go. Isabelle was looking in the mirror and I couldn't help but stare at her.

She didn't even look away from the mirror when she said, "You're staring again."

I just chuckled and smiled. "I know." I could never take my eyes off my beautiful wife. Huh, I like saying that. Matter of fact I love saying that. Mrs. Mitchell.

She turned to look at me and smiled with a twinkle in her eye like she knew exactly what I was thinking. I pulled her closer to me and nestled my head on top of hers. "So, Mrs. Mitchell, are you ready? Ready for the honeymoon? To be married? To be with me forever?"

She started to laugh. "You have no idea."

Epilogue

3 years later

Ryder

"YOU MOTHERFUCKING SON OF A BITCH!" Isabelle was screaming at the top of her lungs and sweating profusely.

I went to the bathroom to dampen a cloth with cold water and wrung it out. I walked back into the room and approached my wife. I put the damp cloth on her forehead and started to wipe away the sweat. "Sweetheart, please calm down, okay? I love you."

Isabelle waved her hands in the air and pushed my hand away from her face. "Oh no! Don't you dare sweetheart me and smile at me all sexy like that! You know what those damn dimples do to me! And don't even get me started on the nipple rings!"

I couldn't help but burst out laughing. Then for the damn life of me I started getting hard thinking about the first time she saw those nipple rings and went batshit crazy on me. "Yeah, sweetheart, I do know what they do to you because of our little situation right now."

I tried to smile at her and then I heard her growl at me. Holy shit! If it were at all possible I was getting harder just hearing her growl at me. *Okay, come on, Ryd, let's think clearly right now. Um, puppies, kittens, kittens that purr, lions and tigers that growl, Isabelle growling ... Okay, not helping at all!*

I shook my head and tried to put the cloth back to her forehead but she pushed it away again and her face got really red. "Don't you da—AH! HOLY SHITBALLS!"

I didn't know how much longer I could take this. I couldn't stand seeing my girl in pain. If I could take her place right now I would. I took her hand in mine and kissed her on the forehead. When I leaned back to get a good look at my beautiful girl, I saw tears welling up in her eyes.

"Sweetheart, what's wrong?" Then the damn floods exploded and came crashing down on me. It didn't matter if her tears were happy or sad, I hated seeing her cry. It nearly killed me.

She started flapping her hands all over the place and then her chin started to quiver when she looked back up at me. "Oh Ryder, I'm so sorry for everything. This is just hurting like a bitch and I'm just being a huge baby. You have no idea how much I love you and how lucky I feel each and every day when I wake up next to you."

Oh, but I knew exactly how lucky she felt. If she even felt half as lucky to be with me as I did to be with her, then I'm the luckiest bastard out there. For the life of me, my eyes started to well up with tears.

Come on, man! Keep it together!

I shook my head a couple of times and moved my hand up to wipe the few tears that fell from her beautiful face. "I love you, Isabelle. Forever."

"Oh, Ryder, I love you, too!" And then I leaned in and kissed her on the lips. After pulling back, I looked into her eyes and smiled. I was thinking about putting the cloth back on her forehead but decided against it because the last couple times didn't work out in my favor. I pulled a chair up next to the bed to sit down when Isabelle said, "Ryder?"

I pushed the chair back and moved closer to the bed. "What is it, sweetheart?"

She looked up at me with a twinkle in her eye and smiled. "Do you mind if I have that wash cloth and some ice chips?" I just laughed and put the cloth back to her forehead and grabbed the ice chips. I thought about just handing her the cup, but put an ice chip in my mouth instead. I saw her mouth droop down but then I moved my head closer to her and her eyes lit up. I kissed her and then opened my mouth and felt her tongue against mine. In an instant the ice chip left my mouth and I moaned. I leaned back and looked into her eyes and winked at her. Of course she blushed.

I heard someone clear their throat. "Um, excuse me, Mr. and Mrs. Mitchell? If it's all right with you, I would like to deliver this baby before you make plans to have another one. You guys think you're up for that?"

I looked back at my wife, and if it was at all possible, her face got even redder. I put my hand to her forehead and wiped away the loose hair, kissed her, and winked at her again. Without taking my eyes off her I said, "Yeah, sorry about that, Dr. Allen. Sweetheart, are you ready?"

I heard her take a few deep breaths and then she nodded her head. "Yeah, let's do this."

Dr. Allen moved in between my wife's legs and sat down. "Okay, Isabelle. On the count of three I'm going to tell you to push. One. Two. Three. Push."

Isabelle was holding onto my hand and I thought it was going to fall off from how hard she held it. She grunted and her face turned bright red. I couldn't help but feel proud to be her husband and to have a child with her. In all the time I knew her, one thing never changed. That Isabelle was a damn good fighter. She pushed a few more times and then I heard the most beautiful sound ever.

A baby crying.

My baby.

Our baby.

My eyes welled up with tears and I looked down at Isabelle, who was looking at me with tears in her eyes. I couldn't believe it. Our little pumpkin was finally here. I leaned down and kissed her on the forehead. "I love you, sweetheart." She kissed me again on the lips before she said, "I love you too, Ryder. So much." I moved back from her and we both smiled at one another and then turned our heads to where the nurses were cleaning our little pumpkin up.

Dr. Allen walked over to shake my hand and kissed Isabelle on the cheek. I would've freaked out, but Dr. Allen was Sarah's stepfather. Dr. Allen had helped deliver their watermelon, Noah, and fell in love with Sarah's mom, Jill. "Congratulations, you two. You have a beautiful, healthy little baby girl." A nurse walked over at that moment carrying a little bundle wrapped in a bright pink blanket and handed her off to my sweetheart.

I was in complete and utter shock. I couldn't believe that my little pumpkin was finally here. I didn't even think I was crying until Isabelle put her hand on my face and wiped the tears away with her thumb and smiled. Damn. That smile could bring me to my knees. It could make me do anything. Be anything. Like getting up at two in the morning to get Isabelle pickle chips because she was craving them. Or when she needed butterscotch frozen yogurt and I had to drive around forever to find it because the frozen yogurt stand was closed. Because it was January.

Her hand was still on my face and I held it there while I kissed her wrist. "I love you, Isabelle. So much." I then put her hand in mine and knelt down to kiss my beautiful wife on the lips and then stared at my little pumpkin.

She kissed me on the cheek and I could feel her smiling against me. "I love you too, Ryder." Our moment was broken when Dr. Allen asked us a very important question. "So guys, what's this beautiful little girl's name?"

I smiled, never taking my eyes off our little pumpkin. I kissed our pumpkin on the forehead and then turned to look at Isabelle, who for once was staring at me. "Are you sure, sweetheart?"

She smiled and nodded her head. "Yes. I don't think I've ever been surer of anything in my entire life. Well, besides marrying you." I smiled and looked to Dr. Allen. "Idea Lynn Mitchell."

Throughout the entire pregnancy we kept trying to think of the most perfect name for our little girl. My pumpkin. Our pumpkin. Sure, there are many beautiful names out there, but we wanted ours to be unique to our situation. I smiled just thinking back on the memory.

***

Lying in bed, I was designing a new tattoo for a customer. Isabelle was in the process of writing her third novel. Her first novel was entitled Ours *and was on the* New York Times *bestseller list for thirteen weeks. Her second was entitled,* Forever, *and was on the list for twenty two weeks.*

Huffing a few times, Isabelle placed the laptop on the stand. Taking a few sips of water, Isabelle turned to me. While rubbing her belly she said, "All right, Ryd. We have got to think of a name for this little one. I'm already seven months pregnant and we don't have that much time left."

While I still drew the tattoo, I smiled. "I have an idea. What if we name her Idea?" My heart was beating erratically. I didn't hear anything for a few seconds so I looked over at her. "Iz?"

With the biggest smile on her face she said, "Idea. It definitely fits." Smiling, Isabelle wrapped her arms around my neck and kissed me.

I pulled her onto my lap so she was straddling me. Isabelle kissed me one last time. "I love it," she whispered, smiling down at me.

Isabelle started to lean in to kiss me but I placed my hands on either side of her face. "I love you," I whispered.

"I love you too, Ryder."

We stared at one another with smiles on our faces before making love.

***

I was smiling when I felt a hand wrap around mine. I looked at Isabelle and she smiled almost as if she knew exactly what I was thinking about. Dr. Allen smiled and wrote the name on the birth certificate and handed us each a pen to give our signatures. "What a beautiful name. Congratulations again, you guys." After we handed him back the birth certificate, he left the delivery room and closed the door behind him.

I smiled again at my two beautiful girls as I sat down on the edge of the bed and wrapped an arm around my sweetheart.

Luck was definitely on my side the day I ran into Isabelle Katherine Clark. Literally.

I looked down to see Idea sucking on her mommy's pinky and I saw the biggest smile come across Isabelle's face. I tried to get a few brown curls under control on Idea's head and then Isabelle kissed her on the forehead. "Idea. Our Idea."

I smiled and then said, "Our beautiful Idea."

The End

Acknowledgments

I can't believe the amazing journey this series has been on. To think this is only the beginning of it is something I can't wrap my head around. Without the support from my family and friends I wouldn't be where I am right now. Every single one of you hold a special place in my heart.

Thank you, Mom, for having the following conversation with me. It means more to me than you will ever know.

Me: This just doesn't happen to normal people.
Mom: Yeah, but you've never been normal.

Josh, thank you for being there for me. Thank you for being my cheerleader, my best friend, my cuddle buddy, and my kissy monster. I love you.

A huge, ginormous thank you to Erica from the bottom of my heart to the depths of my soul for being there for me every step of the way!

Alessandra, thank you for helping me and making this at times difficult process just a little bit easier.

Thank you to Limitless Publishing for taking a major chance on me, especially Jennifer O' Neill and Jessica Gunhammer.

Toni Rakestraw for editing, Robin Harper of *Wicked by Design,* for the beautiful covers, and Dixie Matthews for formatting, a big thank you!

And last but certainly not least, thank you to all of the readers. Old and new. I am deeply grateful and humbled by this amazing experience. Thank you for taking time out of your busy and hectic lives of kids, work, etc. to read my books. This all started with an idea and I cannot believe it became a reality ... my reality.

XoXo, Emily

About the Author

For the past 21 years, I have been a planner and an organizer. I always needed things a specific way and then everything changed for me. I've always had a vivid imagination and thoughts racing through my mind. I realized that life is way too short to let things pass me by, because in the blink of an eye everything could change. So I decided to just live in the moment, taking every chance and opportunity led my way. No second thoughts and just going with the flow.

I decided to put the fictional characters and the conversations going on in my head to paper. I know, it makes me sound crazy, but I wouldn't have it any other way. I've embraced crazy and hectic and last minute because it's led me to making my dreams a reality.

When I'm not writing Happily Ever Afters I'm reading about them and living one. I think this world is filled with too much sadness already we don't need to read about it as well. I write because I love it and I've allowed my imagination to run wild and be crazy and free. Just like me.

Contact Emily:

Facebook:
https://www.facebook.com/pages/Emily-McKee/1411551212390451

Twitter:
https://twitter.com/EmilyMcKee1206

Goodreads:
http://www.goodreads.com/author/show/7079840.Emily_McKee

Amazon:
http://www.amazon.com/Emily-McKee/e/B00DE3QVGW

Made in the
USA
Monee, IL